DEDICATION

To my editor, Caroline Creahan, for her intuition and never-ending help with making my stories become the best they can be. Thank you!

LOVE FOUND

Pack Law 6

Becca Van

MENAGE EVERLASTING

Siren Publishing, Inc.
www.SirenPublishing.com

A SIREN PUBLISHING BOOK
IMPRINT: Ménage Everlasting

LOVE FOUND
Copyright © 2013 by Becca Van

ISBN: 978-1-62242-707-9

First Printing: March 2013

Cover design by Les Byerley
All art and logo copyright © 2013 by Siren Publishing, Inc.

Printed in the U.S.A.

PUBLISHER
Siren Publishing, Inc.
www.SirenPublishing.com

LOVE FOUND

Pack Law 6

BECCA VAN
Copyright © 2013

Chapter One

"Bye, Rylan! Thanks for lunch!"

Rylan Friess lifted his head from his work and managed a smile for Samantha Domain and Talia Friess as they waved from the doorway. He shifted his gaze along the booths, where the two women's mates were standing around and talking.

Thank goodness.

He knew he ought to be pleased that his pack mates were supporting the club. Samantha's mates, Roan, Chet, and Justin, had managed the Aztec Club before handing over the reins to Rylan and his brothers. He appreciated that they would come eat here, but watching the mated couples together for the past hour had been surprisingly painful.

"My pleasure," he said to Samantha. "Where are you off to now?"

"The boys are dropping us off to get our nails done," Talia answered. "The babies are home with Cindy and Angela, so we're having a girls' day. Michelle is treating."

Rylan smiled as he pictured little Stefan, his Alphas' and queen's son, as he had demanded attention from anyone who had been willing to give it as he'd toddled from person to person the previous evening. His big cousins Justin, Roan, and Chet Domain, with their mate and wife, Samantha, had cooed over their three-month-old baby boy, Tristan.

"Tell my queen I said hello," Rylan answered respectfully.

Her mates having joined her at the door, Talia was on the point of leaving, but she turned and raised an eyebrow at Rylan. "I'm not repeating that 'my queen' stuff to her. You know she doesn't like it."

Rylan's brother Tarkyn spoke up from behind him, his tone teasing. "But it befits her royal queenliness."

Samantha rolled her eyes. "'Queenliness' isn't even a word."

Rylan watched his brother lean on the bar and grin. He didn't have it in him to smile and banter right now, but that was never Tarkyn's problem.

Hearing footsteps behind him, he turned and found his youngest brother, Chevy, coming up the stairs from the storage room, a case of beer in his hands. As Tarkyn and the two women continued to tease each other, Chevy glanced between them, and then his gaze darted to Rylan. More patient and cautious than Rylan, Chevy looked like he was wondering if Tarkyn ought to be trading jokes with women whose mates were so protective of them.

Chet Domain wrapped his arm around Samantha's waist. "Let's go, baby," he said.

Samantha snuggled into Chet's touch and happily directed her teasing at him instead. "What, are you going to use your 'voice' on me?"

"Maybe I will," Chet answered with a playful growl. His arm still around her, they went out.

Rylan watched them go, feeling conflicted. He was happy for all those in the pack who had found their mates, but he wanted to share that joy, not watch it from the outside. Lunch today had brought the two sets of Betas, men who were powerful within the pack and happily mated, out with their women. By comparison, Rylan and his brothers might not be eligible for the honor of becoming Betas for years. As for finding their mate, that might never happen at all.

The others filed out as well, the men touching their women with the blend of possessiveness and affection that was the hallmark of a werewolf in love. When the door closed behind the last of them, Rylan let out the breath he'd been holding.

"I appreciate the business," Chevy said, loading beer into the fridge, "but I kind of wish the Domains would show their approval some other way."

Even Tarkyn's smile had disappeared. "You're just jealous," he said, his eyes still locked on the door.

"We all are." Rylan made himself put his mind to work. "Deliveries here yet?" he asked Chevy.

"Should be any moment." Chevy closed the fridge door. He glanced at Tarkyn, who still looked moody. "We'll get our turn eventually."

Rylan didn't answer. Not everyone did get a turn at true love. And even if a wolf found his mate, he had to woo her…

"Not soon enough," Tarkyn complained.

"You just have to be pa…" Chevy stopped. "What's that smell?"

Rylan inhaled deeply. The sweetest, most delectable scent he'd ever encountered assailed his nostrils. The aroma was wafting through the open door to the storage room and up the stairs.

He glanced at Tarkyn and Chevy, who had frozen and were also sniffing.

"What is…" Tarkyn began only to halt as a low growl rumbled up from his chest.

"Mate!" Rylan practically snarled and headed to the basement stairs. He descended them and strode across the storage room toward the ramp leading down from the open outer doors before he even knew he was going to move. His brothers were right behind him. Glancing around the room quickly and using his wolf's enhanced eyesight, he was disappointed to find the basement empty. He moved stealthily toward the outside doors then halted in his tracks at the bottom of the ramp, which sloped up to where the delivery trucks parked outside, when the silhouette of a woman was showcased by the sunlight shining from behind her.

"Um, hi, I was just bringing the last of the delivery," she said as she rolled the hand truck down the sloping concrete ramp and stopped halfway. He was a little frustrated that he couldn't see all of her. He could make out the color of her hair, but the sun was still making it difficult for him to see. Then he took a step forward as she took another few steps down the ramp. His breath hitched in his throat and his heart stuttered. She was the most beautiful woman he had ever seen, and he wanted to pick her up, carry her to his truck, and take her back to the pack house and then spend hours buried inside her body. When the muscles in her body tensed with wariness he exhaled and then drew in a deep breath. He wanted to know everything about her. She wheeled the dolly the rest of the way down the ramp, and he stepped aside to give her room. The last thing he wanted to do was crowd her and make her even more skittish.

"Who are you?" Rylan asked.

"Uh, um, my name is Alyson Redding. I'm filling in for Shawn. He's on vacation."

"Let me do that for you." Tarkyn moved in close and took the trolley handle from Alyson and then pushed it down the rest of the way.

"Uh, thanks, but that's my job."

"How long have you been working for the delivery company, Alyson?" Tarkyn asked, ignoring her statement.

"Um, two weeks." She looked from Rylan to Chevy and Tarkyn then back to Rylan.

"I'm being rude." He moved forward and held his hand out toward her. "I'm Rylan Friess and these are my brothers, Tarkyn and Chevy. We manage the club."

"Pleased to meet you." Alyson took his hand. A growl threatened to rumble up from his chest, but Rylan swallowed it down and pushed at his wolf. His skin tingled where their hands connected, and his beast was pushing at him to claim his mate. Alyson's eyes widened, and she practically snatched her hand back. She must have felt the electricity sparking between them, too. Excitement permeated his body that she had felt the connection he did. Just when he and his brothers had been feeling so down after watching their cousins and pack members with their women their own mate had shown up. The sexual pull toward her was like nothing he'd ever felt before. All the women who had been in his life previously paled to nonexistence in comparison, and he was finding it hard to control his wolf. Her scent was driving him insane and his cock was rapidly filling with blood and his balls were aching.

"Do you live locally, Alyson?" Tarkyn asked as he unloaded the cases of beer.

"I live in Bloomfield." She walked over to where Tarkyn was just placing another case of beer onto a stack and reached out to pick one up.

"No. Let Tarkyn do it." Rylan placed a hand on her shoulder.

"But…"

"Why don't you come upstairs for a drink?" Rylan guided her toward the stairs on the opposite side of the room with a hand to her lower back. He didn't want her running off now that she had finished delivering their order. He wanted to spend as much time with her as possible.

"Oh, but…"

"We have coffee," Chevy said from behind them.

"Coffee sounds good."

Rylan studied Alyson surreptitiously. Although she was tall for a woman, standing at around five ten, she wasn't as big as he and his brothers were. Her head only came up to his shoulder, and to him she was just about perfect. He and his brothers were all big men, but the thought of having Alyson up against his body made his half-hard dick engorge so quickly, it jerked painfully against his zipper. She would fit perfectly between him and his brothers without being overwhelmed by their size. All of them were over six and a half feet. He was glad that their mate wasn't small like some women. When he and his brothers eventually got her into their bed, he wouldn't have to be afraid of crushing her.

Not only was Alyson tall, she was gorgeous, with her long black hair pulled back into a braid. Even in a braid, her hair reached to the top of her ass. Rylan wanted to release her hair and spread it out. He could almost imagine what it would feel like caressing his naked flesh. Pushing his wayward thoughts aside and his eager animal back down, he entered the door off the bar.

"Have a seat, Alyson. I'll get that coffee."

He returned with a tray bearing four coffee mugs as well as cream and sugar. Alyson looked pretty sitting on a stool at the bar. Her skin was pale but clear of any blemishes except for a small mole off to the right side of her mouth. Her lower lip was lusciously full, and the top, although thinner, was perfectly bowed. And her eyes…If he looked too long into those violet pools, he might just lose himself. He'd never seen such beautifully colored irises before, and her eyes were tilted slightly up at the outer corners, almost feline in shape. They were framed by the longest, thickest, darkest eyelashes he'd ever seen. She didn't wear any makeup or perfume, for which his wolf was grateful. She had on a pair of tight hip-hugging jeans and a tank top. The muscles in her arms bulged slightly, a testament to the heavy lifting she did for her job.

"Thanks." Alyson accepted the mug of coffee and then sipped appreciatively.

Chevy and Tarkyn had already claimed the stools on either side of her, so Rylan stayed behind the bar and watched her. She brushed a stray hair from her face, the move so feminine he was almost enthralled. Her violet eyes connected with his, and her skin flushed before she quickly looked away.

"How long have you lived in Bloomfield, Alyson?" Chevy asked.

"Uh, not long," she hedged.

"How long is Shawn on leave for?" Tarkyn sipped his coffee as he watched Alyson intently.

"I'm not sure, but I think he's on a long vacation."

Good, Rylan thought. The longer Shawn was away, the more he and his brothers would hopefully see of Alyson.

"Will you be doing all the deliveries here while Shawn is on vacation?" Chevy asked.

Alyson shrugged her shoulders. The movement made her breasts move and drew Rylan's attention to her chest. He wondered what color her nipples were and if they would be sensitive. She had nice breasts, not too large and not too small. They would fit perfectly into his large hands. Rylan ground his teeth together. He had to get control of his emotions and desires. The last thing he wanted to do was scare Alyson off before they'd had the chance to woo her. Lifting his eyes from her chest, he was thankful to see she was still looking at Chevy and hadn't noticed his perusal of her body.

"I think so, but I can't ever be too sure. I deliver where my boss, Jerry, tells me to."

"What made you get into this line of work?" Tarkyn drew Alyson's gaze.

She didn't answer immediately, looking from Tarkyn to Chevy. "You guys sure do ask a lot of questions."

"Back off," Chevy urged Rylan and Tarkyn telepathically.

"And I thought you two were unloading the delivery," Alyson added to Tarkyn and Chevy.

"All taken care of," Tarkyn answered.

"It's a small town, baby," Rylan said, hoping to put her at ease. "We're just being friendly."

Alyson didn't look like she was buying it. Shrugging, she answered Tarkyn's question. "I needed a job and this one was available."

"What did you do before?" Rylan leaned his hip against the edge of the bar.

Alyson looked wary and uncertain, not meeting his gaze. She studied her mug of coffee and wrapped her hands around the cup. "Oh, I just sort of flittered from job to job. Nothing grand."

Rylan inhaled deeply. He scented fear and the light fragrance from her soap or bodywash but also the faint tinge of her womanly scent. She met his eyes and caught him watching her. Alyson's cheeks colored a slight pink hue and as she nervously shifted on the stool, the sweet aroma of her arousal assailed his nostrils. It seemed Alyson felt the sexual attraction as much as he and his brothers did, but he pushed that knowledge aside for now. What concerned him most right at this minute was the essence of her fear. That he didn't like one little bit.

"*Our mate is scared,*" Tarkyn said through their private mental link.

"*I'm aware. What I'd like to know is what she is afraid of and why she lied about her previous employment,*" Rylan said.

"*How do you know she's lying?*" Chevy asked.

"*She keeps looking away and shifting nervously,*" Rylan explained.

"*That could be because we're strangers to her.*" Chevy narrowed his eyes at Rylan.

"*Use your wolf senses, Chevy. You can smell the anxiety coming off of her.*" Tarkyn took a sip of his coffee.

"*I was trying to keep my wolf at bay. It's pushing at me to claim our mate. If I don't keep a tight rein on my beast, I'm afraid Alyson will notice we're different.*"

"*Fuck!*" Tarkyn shot an agitated look to Alyson. "*How the hell are we going to keep her here with us?*"

"*We aren't,*" Rylan replied. "*It's way too soon. We need to get to know her better first. She's so nervous and anxious right now that if we push too hard, she won't come back.*"

"*I think we should place more orders,*" Tarkyn suggested. "*We'll have to run it by the Alphas, but if we schedule in smaller regular orders instead of one big one, we can see her every day.*"

"You are a sneaky bastard, Tarkyn." Rylan smiled. *"I like the way your mind works. If Alyson has to come here every day, then she will definitely get to know us and hopefully become more comfortable with us."*

"I don't think our Alphas will have a problem with us changing the order schedule." Chevy looked over at Alyson. *"The amounts delivered won't change, just the regularity."*

"So, how long have you all worked here?" Alyson asked, looking at them with a frown as if trying to work out why they had been so quiet.

"We've been here nearly twelve months." Tarkyn shifted on his stool. "We took over the running of the club when our cousins Justin, Roan, and Chet found—were promoted."

"You grew up in Aztec?"

"Yes." Rylan placed his empty coffee mug on the bar. "Our whole family lives in this town. Since we all do business together and we're close relations, we all share a large house not far out of town. We each have our own suite of rooms though, which gives us privacy when we need it. But we like to hang out with our brothers and cousins."

"Must be nice," Alyson muttered under her breath and looked down at the bar.

She frowned, and a wistful expression crossed her face. Chevy opened his mouth, but Rylan shook his head slightly, stopping his brother before he could ask her about her family.

"Thanks for the coffee, but I need to get moving." Alyson edged off the stool, careful not to touch Chevy or Tarkyn, and headed around the end of the bar toward the inside stairs. "Do you want me to close the outside door?"

Rylan had already stepped out from behind the bar to follow her, but as she asked her question she stopped and turned, slamming right into him. She drew in a deep, shaky breath, her cheeks flushed once more, and she quickly stepped back from him. Rylan moved lightning fast and grabbed her hips just as her back foot met air. A slight squeak left her mouth, and then he pulled her up against his body, safely away from the stairs. She leaned her head on his chest and panted for air, rolling her forehead over his pectoral muscle. Her body stiffened, and she stepped sideways.

"Thanks for stopping me from falling. See ya." Alyson spun around and jogged down the stairs.

Rylan didn't follow her this time but watched her from the top. She rushed over to her dolly and then hurried up the ramp, pulling it behind her and muttering to herself the whole way. The outside doors slammed closed, and then she was gone.

"Fuck, she's a skittish little thing." Chevy stood up and adjusted his dick in his pants.

"Yeah, she is," Tarkyn agreed, "but she smells so damn sweet. I'm so hard I think my balls have turned blue."

Rylan unclipped his cell and dialed. "Hi, Jonah, I was wondering if you would be averse to us making a few changes to the delivery schedule for the club."

"What do you have in mind?" Jonah Friess, one of his Alphas, asked, and Rylan was glad his brothers had enhanced hearing so he wouldn't have to repeat the conversation. They had their heads tilted to the side slightly as they listened intently.

"We just met our mate. Her name is Alyson, and she made the delivery to the club," Rylan began to explain.

Jonah laughed. "Congratulations, cousins. It's about damn time, and you can do what you like with the delivery orders. I may be your Alpha, but we are family. You do whatever you have to and get to know your mate."

"Thanks, Jonah." Rylan disconnected the call. "Tarkyn, get on the computer and change our orders."

Tarkyn smiled and took off for the office at a near sprint. Rylan sighed, but inside he was just as eager as his impatient younger brother to see Alyson again.

Chapter Two

What the hell just happened? Alyson sat in the driver's seat of the small delivery truck and sighed. *Why was I attracted to three men? God! What is wrong with me?* She groaned and leaned over until her head touched the steering wheel. Taking a deep breath, she turned on the ignition and pulled out of the parking lot.

When she had sat on that barstool sipping her coffee, it had felt like those three men could see into her soul. She'd never felt such an instant connection to anyone before. It was damned disconcerting. She shivered and moisture leaked onto her panties at the remembered heat of each Friess brother's touch.

Damn it, Alyson, get your head out of the clouds. You are already in a world of trouble, and you don't need a relationship to complicate matters further.

Alyson concentrated on her driving as she thought over her reaction to Rylan, Tarkyn, and Chevy. She'd never been interested in a man before, let alone three men. Her previous line of work had made her wary in regards to the opposite sex. Of course she'd mucked around a bit in college, but she'd never gone the whole nine yards. Men were jerks and couldn't be trusted. God knew she'd seen that time and again after graduating.

Chevy, Tarkyn, and Rylan might have caught her eye, but their questions had unnerved her. Six months working her way across Arizona and into New Mexico had taught her to hide her secrets well, but it was as if they knew when she was fibbing. *I should keep running.* The handsome club owners weren't the first enticement for her to stay in this area. For some reason she'd stopped running when she'd reached Bloomfield. It wasn't just that moving from town to town was as hard on her nerves as it was on her body. Something about the quiet town had called to her. So five months ago she had leased a fully furnished bungalow attached to the back of an elderly couple's house and worked at odd jobs until this one came up. She had only been working for Jerry for two weeks, and even though she was still getting to know the cantankerous older man, she liked him, a lot. He was like the father figure she'd never had.

Jerry was gruff but fair, and if he didn't like something, he wasn't shy about letting you know. Alyson liked to know where she stood. The thought of trying to read between lines just irritated and frustrated her. If she'd done something wrong, she wanted to know about it so she could change or fix whatever her transgression was.

Alyson tugged on the steering wheel slightly when the front wheel touched the edge of the gravel. She sighed and pushed all those disconcerting thoughts aside and concentrated on her driving. Jerry would blow a gasket if she got in an accident.

Twelve minutes later she was pulling the truck into the large warehouse. After turning off the ignition, she hopped out of the driver's seat.

"Alyson," Jerry called from his office door, "come into my office."

Oh shit! Have I done something wrong? Jerry was scowling as usual, but there seemed to be an underlying tension around his mouth. *Did I take too long making the delivery? Did the Friess brothers complain about me? Maybe I should have been more persistent when Tarkyn took the hand truck from me.*

Alyson hurried across the blue-painted concrete floor and into Jerry's office.

"Take a seat." He waved his hand toward the chair across from his desk. "The Aztec Club has changed their delivery schedule."

Is he studying me more intently than normal? Alyson tried to keep her face blank and her body still. It took more effort than she would have thought when the sexy image of the Friess brothers flashed through her mind.

"Okay," Alyson said, and even though she wanted to ask questions, she decided silence would be more prudent. If the Friess brothers had something against her, she wasn't about to open her mouth to help get herself in trouble. She needed this job to put food on the table and keep a roof over her head. Her last job hadn't paid much, and she was always living from paycheck to paycheck. Maybe one day she would have enough money to start her own business and work for herself, but she couldn't see that happening in the near future.

"You are to make smaller deliveries daily and a larger one on Saturday afternoon," Jerry said.

"But…" She hesitated.

"Go on and say it," Jerry said gruffly.

"That doesn't make sense. Why would they want smaller deliveries done every day when it would be cheaper to have one larger one done every week? They'll be paying extra for the man hours and fuel."

Jerry studied her, and then she saw a glimmer of amusement in his eyes. She watched with fascination as a smile slowly spread across his mouth and he tipped his head back and let rip with a deep belly laugh. Alyson had no idea what was so funny but smiled anyway. She'd never seen Jerry smile or laugh. His humor seemed to lighten his whole gruff exterior. Finally with a last chuckle he looked at her and grinned as her smile turned to a frown.

"Don't worry about it, sweetheart. If the customer wants their deliveries done every day and is willing to pay for it, why question it? The customer is always right. Your last delivery every day will be to the Aztec Club. By the time you finish up, the warehouse will be closed, so you may as well take the truck home with you."

"You realize that I will have to park it out on the street, don't you? I don't have a garage or driveway I can secure your truck in."

"You live in Bloomfield, sweetheart, not New York. The truck will be fine." Jerry smiled again.

Alyson eyed him and wondered what was going on. Jerry was up to something. She just hadn't figured out what yet.

"Since it's only twenty minutes until knock-off time and there are no more deliveries today, why don't you go on home?"

"Don't you want me to wash the truck first?" Alyson frowned at her boss. He was a stickler about using any free time in the afternoon to keep the company vehicles clean. He sure was acting strange.

"No. Take the time while you can. I have a feeling you aren't going to get any more free time. By the way, you're no longer on probation. You do good work, kid."

"Thanks, Jerry." Alyson rose to her feet and gave Jerry one last look, but he didn't seem to intend to explain. She headed for the door. "See you tomorrow."

* * * *

Chevy answered the phone in the office, kicking the door shut to muffle the music and voices from the front of the club.

"Aztec Club, Chevy speaking."

"Chevy, Jerry here."

Chevy grinned even though the man on the other end of the line couldn't see him. The old wolf had called back just like he'd promised. Chevy asked at once, "What did she say?"

"She's pretty confused over the change to the delivery schedule. She didn't argue, but that's not to say she won't figure out something's up. She's not stupid, you know."

"I never thought she was, Jerry." Chevy sat down on the edge of the desk. "What do you mean 'confused'? She wasn't annoyed, right?"

Jerry sighed. "If she's really your mate, pup, you have bigger problems than whether or not she minds driving out to Aztec every afternoon."

Jerry was a lone werewolf but had been under the Friess Pack's protection for years. Jonah, Mikhail, and Brock's father hadn't wanted a lone wolf in his territory, and when he had tried to get Jerry to join his pack, the man had adamantly refused. But Jerry and Jonah's father had become great friends and had often socialized together before Jonah's dad had handed the Alpha role of the pack over to his three sons. Jerry had become an honorary Friess Pack member from then on.

That meant that Jerry was no stranger to the idea of mating. Better still, he could fill Chevy and his brothers in on their mate.

"So, what can you tell us about Alyson Redding?"

"Not much. She's only been working for me for two weeks, although she has been in town for around five months. She's a feisty, confident woman and a very hard worker. She never gives me any trouble."

"Where is she from?"

"Now, that I don't know. I never asked her."

"Did you ask for any references when she applied for a job?"

"What for?" Jerry asked abruptly. "Someone with half a brain could do the work."

"What is she scared of?"

"Ah, so you picked that up, too. I have no idea, pup, and didn't think it was my place to question her. You and your brothers are going to have your work cut out for you. Underneath that pretty, sassy exterior is a heart of gold, but I also think she has a backbone of steel."

"Okay, well, if you find out what she's so frightened of, you let us know. It is our right to protect our mate." He hated the idea of Alyson being in any danger, so much so that he wished she were back in the club right now. "And make sure that there are no hiccups with our late-afternoon deliveries."

"Hey, don't tell me how to run my business, pup. I was working long before you were a gleam in your father's eye."

"No disrespect intended, Jerry. I'm just eager to see and get to know our mate."

"You be careful with her, Chevy. She's a sweet girl and I don't want to see her hurt."

"We have no intention of hurting our mate," Chevy replied in a growly voice.

"Oh, I know that, but I also know your brothers. Rylan can be such an arrogant bastard."

"Hey, we're wolves, what do you expect?"

Jerry chuckled. "Take care of my girl."

Chevy disconnected the call and went in search of his brothers. They were serving patrons at the bar, and since there were humans about he decided to speak to them using their telepathic link. He told them about his conversation with Jerry and how Alyson's boss was protective of her even though he didn't know her that well.

"Did you ask him if he knew what she was frightened of?" Rylan asked.

"Yeah, he has no idea." Chevy joined his brothers, pulling a beer for one of their patrons.

"We are going to have to get our mate to open up with us." Tarkyn stood at the back of the bar, polishing glasses with a frown on his face. *"We can't protect her if we don't know what we're protecting her from."*

"You're getting ahead of yourself, Tarkyn," Chevy told him. He delivered the beer to their customer with a smile before continuing. *"We have to take things slow with her. We need to give Alyson time to get to know us first."*

Tarkyn glanced up from his work long enough to give Chevy an annoyed look. *"You think I don't know that? Fuck! I just want to hold her and take her back to the den house with us. At least we know she'd be safe there."*

"You think she's in danger?" Chevy asked.

"I'm not sure, but something isn't right."

"I don't like that she's so far away from us," Rylan said as he made change and gave it to one of the humans at the bar. *"But Jerry's right that we have bigger problems than getting her to come see us."*

Tarkyn looked alert. *"Like what?"*

"Like our status in the pack. How is she going to feel that her mates aren't even Betas?"

Chevy sighed aloud, realizing belatedly that the woman he was serving was giving him a funny look. He smiled tightly and turned away. There was no sense trying to tell Rylan that in time they would rise within the pack. They were younger than their cousins, and Jonah and the other Alphas had respected that in promoting the Domain brothers first. If they kept their noses to the grindstone and served the pack well, they'd be treated the same way.

But Rylan was, in his way, just as impatient as Tarkyn, and he felt his lower status in the pack keenly.

"She's human, Ry," Tarkyn said. *"She won't even know what an Alpha is."*

Rylan lifted his eyes to the door. *"Speaking of..."*

Chevy glanced toward the door to see his Alphas and their mate come in. He nodded respectfully, rounded the end of the bar, and then followed them to the booth.

"What can I get you all to drink?" Chevy took their orders and was about to return to the bar when his queen stopped him by placing a hand on his arm. Jonah, Mikhail, and Brock growled low in their throats. Chevy hid his smile. He knew how protective they were of their woman, and now he understood why. He felt the same way about Alyson.

Michelle glared at her men but slowly withdrew her hand from his arm. "Chevy, is your mate here?"

"No, she lives in Bloomfield, but she will be here every afternoon from now on."

"Just let me know if you need my help explaining everything to her, but make sure you get to know her first before you reveal who you are. Don't do what these boneheads did and scare the crap out of her."

"Thank you, my qu...Michelle. I'll be right back with your drinks."

Chevy filled his Alphas' orders. *"What did they say about Alyson?"* Rylan asked.

"Nothing. Michelle wants to help." The look Chevy gave his brother was pointed. *"They're not the enemy, Rylan."*

"I know that! They're our Alphas, and they're good men." Rylan's gaze drifted to the table. *"Jonah seemed happy that we found her, but what if they don't accept her once they meet her? I won't choose between my mate and my pack."*

"You won't have to," Chevy assured him, but he took the drinks back to the Alphas' table in a pensive frame of mind. He found himself studying Michelle as he took their orders for dinner. Michelle was the perfect mate to their leaders. When she had first arrived in Aztec she had seemed shy and introverted, but meeting the Alphas had brought out her true nature. She was a very caring woman, but she was also very strong minded, and she stood up to them like no one else could. Just what the pack and their leaders needed.

Alyson seemed to have some of that feistiness, too, but the way she hid her past from them made Chevy worry. Neither Rylan nor Tarkyn would be patient enough to let her come to them. They'd push her, and Chevy could only hope that his brothers' arrogant dominance didn't scare her away.

Chapter Three

Alyson's stomach was doing a nervous dance. The closer she got to Aztec the worse her stomach churned. For some reason she felt drawn to the three Friess brothers who ran the Aztec Club, but she couldn't for the life of her work out why. She'd never really been interested in men or relationships, because she had seen how women and children had suffered at the hands of so many assholes. Logically she knew she was being unfair by categorizing the Friess brothers with those evil bastards, but it wasn't easy to ignore her experience.

Taking a deep breath, she pulled the small truck into the rear parking lot of the club and reversed as close to the cellar doors as possible. Just as she turned off the ignition and got out, the large wooden doors to the cellar burst open. Rylan walked out and over to the rear of the truck, pulling the tailgate down and extracting her hand cart from the back.

"What are you doing?"

"I'm helping you."

"Look." Alyson frowned and placed her hands on her hips. "I appreciate the help, but this is my job. It's what I get paid for. I can't expect Jerry to pay me if you do my work."

"Don't worry about it." Rylan began to pull cases of beer from the truck and stack them on the cart.

Alyson sighed, and when she picked up another case of beer, warm hands settled on her hips.

"Let me take that, honey."

Alyson glared at Tarkyn as he stepped around her and took the box from her hands. She stood back and watched with frustrated exasperation as the two arrogant men did her work.

"You can't stay out here. Don't you have customers to serve?"

"They're being well taken care of, sweetie."

Alyson jumped at the deep voice close behind her. She half turned and had to crane her neck to look up into Chevy's green eyes. He was a big man and had to stand around six foot six. The sun was shining brightly and highlighted the lighter streaks in his brown hair. As he joined his brothers in unloading cases of beer from the truck, his biceps bulged as did his massive pectoral muscles. Cream dripped from her pussy, dampening her panties, and it wasn't until Chevy smirked at her that she realized she was staring.

"Why don't you come on into the bar and have a drink, Alyson?" Chevy didn't wait for her reply. He just gripped her arm gently and began to lead her down the ramp into the cellar.

"Uh, I don't…"

"Don't tell me you don't have time. I know we're your last delivery for the day."

His words made her wonder if he and his brothers had arranged for them to be the last delivery on her list. *Nah, you're imagining things, Alyson. Why would they care what time their order is delivered? But why did they change to daily deliveries rather than having one large one every week?*

"What are you thinking so hard about, sweetie?" Chevy asked as he led her across the concrete floor to the internal stairs.

"Nothing much." She shrugged.

Chevy sat on the barstool next to her and nodded to the young man behind the bar. The bartender bowed his head to Chevy and then did the same to Rylan and Tarkyn as they walked behind the mahogany counter. *What's with that?* She watched as he moved down to the other end and began serving a group of very large men. *What do they put in the water here? Growth hormones?*

"What can I get you, baby?" Rylan asked.

"I'll just have a sparkling water, thanks. And my name is Alyson."

"Oh, I know your name."

A high-pitched, saccharine voice asked, "How about my name, Rylan?"

Alyson turned and saw a redheaded woman leaning on the end of the bar. She gave Rylan a simpering smile.

It shouldn't have surprised Alyson that men as good looking as the Friess brothers would attract female attention, but annoyance surged through her. *Who does that redheaded chick think she is?*

"Hi, Cherry," Rylan said distractedly. Tarkyn had just shouted a drink order at him, and he filled it busily.

That didn't stop Cherry, who sidled down the bar and put herself too close to Rylan and flipped her hair over her shoulder. "Need a hand?" she purred.

"What?" Rylan looked at her like she'd appeared out of nowhere. "No. Thanks, Cherry. Don't you have tables?"

That's right. Keep away from them. Alyson stopped herself, surprised. *Girl, they're not yours any more than they're hers.*

That didn't stop her from feeling satisfied as Cherry slunk away, pouting.

Tarkyn came around the bar and took the other seat beside her. Just like yesterday, she thought, mystified. Why did they keep putting themselves so close to her? If women like Cherry were throwing themselves at the Friess brothers, they'd surely have no interest in Alyson.

Rylan helped the other guy serve more customers, but she caught him watching her as he prepared the drinks. When he was done, he walked down the bar and positioned himself right in front of her. He leaned on his elbows and looked her straight in the eye.

Alyson shifted in her seat nervously. Feeling a little intimidated at being surrounded by such large men, she began to wring her fingers together. She could feel the heat emanating from Tarkyn and Chevy on either side of her. Their colognes drifted to her nose. They smelled so good it took all her effort not to groan out loud.

Think about something else.

Swiveling on her stool, Alyson studied the building and the patrons. There were only a couple of exceptions, but most of the men were all muscular, handsome, and tall. When a couple of men smiled and winked at her, she glared back. Low, rumbling growls sounded from beside and behind her. Startled, she eyed Rylan, Tarkyn, and Chevy. They were all frowning at her.

"Did you all just growl at me?" she asked, scowling at each of them.

"Uh, you don't want to encourage any of the men in here, baby," Rylan stated. "They can be a little aggressive."

Alyson just raised her eyebrow and gave him the look that usually froze men in their tracks as she took a sip of her drink. Rylan stared back at her until she finally looked away. It pissed her off that she hadn't been able to hold his gaze, but for some reason she'd let him stare her down. Although she didn't know him, she could tell he was full of arrogance. He stood leaning against the bar with his arms crossed over his chest, but he hadn't taken his eyes off of her. Her body was reacting to the three men close by, and that just pissed her off more. Her breasts felt heavy and swollen and her pussy leaked continuously.

Movement to her side drew her attention, and she surreptitiously watched Tarkyn from beneath her lowered eyelashes. He leaned in toward her slightly and inhaled deeply. A groan rumbled up from his chest and he closed his eyes.

Did he just sniff me?

"You smell good, honey."

Alyson gasped. "What did you say?"

Tarkyn slowly spun around on his seat and leaned in toward her until his nose was against her neck. Alyson froze. "I said you smell good."

Okay, this place is weird. The men were all gigantic, that bartender had bowed to the Friess brothers, and now Tarkyn was sniffing her neck. She refused to acknowledge the shiver of arousal that moved through her at his words and the low growl of his voice. She needed to be wary of these men, not turned on by them.

"I don't need this shit." She put her glass down on the bar and slid from her stool. Instead of walking toward the internal stairs, which would have brought her too close to Tarkyn, she headed for the front doors. Just as she pushed the doors open, a large arm wrapped around her waist. *How did he get to me so quickly?*

Alyson debated whether to cause a scene or to let Rylan pull her back into the club. She decided on the latter. But Rylan didn't just seat her back on the barstool. He lifted her into his arms and carried her to another door near the bar. He walked down a long hallway and then into a large office without breaking a sweat. She had known by his bulging muscles he was strong, but she was astounded that he had no trouble carrying her. Although the show of strength turned her on, she felt vulnerable.

Rylan sat down on a sofa, taking her with him, and secured her on his lap with his arms wrapped around her waist. He withdrew one arm and then shifted her so she was sitting sideways across his thighs until she could see his face as well as Tarkyn's and Chevy's. They had followed Rylan down the hallway and into the office, too. Chevy walked over to one of the desks and leaned against it, while Tarkyn walked toward her.

Tarkyn squatted down in front of them, gently clasped her chin, and scowled at her. "What is wrong with you? Why did you get in a huff because I complimented you? Did you think I was lying?"

Alyson didn't want to admit that she wasn't used to so much male attention. She had thought he was just complimenting her as an effort to get into her panties. But now that he was looking at her so intently, she could see he was feeling a little hurt and a lot pissed off.

"I don't know you." She pushed his hand away from her chin and tried to get off Rylan's lap, but he only tightened his arm around her midsection.

"Tell me you don't feel a connection to us, Alyson," Rylan said, and even though she didn't want to look at him she found herself gazing into his eyes.

"Will you please let me up?" Alyson asked and shoved against his shoulder. She wasn't used to being touched and most of the time didn't like it. *So why do I like it when Rylan, Tarkyn, and Chevy are close? Why do I want them to touch me more?*

Tarkyn stood up and moved back a few paces, and Rylan released her. Alyson gained her feet and stepped away from them, giving herself some room to breathe. It felt like all the air in the room was being sucked up by the three men watching her. She walked around the edge of the room and sat down behind one of the large desks, which put her behind Chevy, so he moved away and slouched against the wall. Having the big piece of wood furniture between her and the Friess brothers slightly eased her tension and that vulnerable feeling.

She eyed the door, but Chevy was leaning against the wall just inside the doorway and she didn't want to take the chance of getting too close to him. He was eyeing her as if she was his next meal.

A quick glance at Rylan and Tarkyn, who was now sitting on the sofa next to his brother, only made her feel more like some large predator's prey, except that, although she was wary and nervous, she wasn't scared. In fact the way they were eying her just seemed to push her long-dead but newly awakened libido higher.

Alyson crossed her legs and squeezed, trying to circumvent the ache in her clit, but that only seemed to make it worse. Her pussy clenched and released a gush of cream onto her already-damp panties. She heard sniffing, and when she looked up it was to see the three men staring at her hungrily.

Can they smell my arousal? No. They're too far away. Get a grip, Alyson.

"You haven't answered any of our questions, Alyson. Are you scared of us?" Tarkyn asked as he pinned her with a stare. She could see the determination in his eyes and didn't know if he or his arrogant ass of a brother, Rylan, would let her get away with avoiding their questions. No one had ever given a damn about her. Why did these men care how she felt?

"No." She finally found her voice and rose to her feet. "I have things to do. I need to get home."

As she made her way to the door, Chevy stepped in front of it and crossed his arms over his massive chest. She halted and stared at him, willing him to move so she could leave. Alyson jumped when large hands clasped her hips. She tried to step out of his grip, but Rylan wouldn't let her.

"You aren't going anywhere until you answer some questions. If and when I am satisfied by your answers, then you may go."

Alyson spun around and knocked his hands off her body. Her breathing was fast and ragged, but not just from anger. These three men got to her in a way she had never experienced before, and she wasn't sure she liked it. She hurried back to the safety of the desk chair, sat down, and glared up at Rylan where he stood in the middle of the room.

"Who the hell do you think you are? You are nothing to me."

Rylan moved forward stealthily. Two steps were all he needed to reach her. He bent and placed his large hands in the middle of the desk, leaning forward.

"Now that's where you're wrong, baby. We are more to you than you could ever know."

What the hell is he talking about?

She watched warily as he leaned over a little further and closed his eyes as he inhaled. When his eyelids moved up again she cringed back in the chair as she stared into his eyes. Instead of their normal blue, they were a deep, glowing gold color. Alyson used her legs to push her chair back until it hit the wall. The jolt that ran through her was enough to pull her from her semi-trance.

"What are you?" she whispered and wrapped her arms around her waist in an unconsciously defensive move.

Rylan blinked and pushed up until he was once more standing upright. He paced a few times and then turned toward her once more. "I will answer your questions once you have answered mine. Now, why did Tarkyn complimenting you make you angry?"

"I never get compliments, and I don't like men," she snapped.

"What?" Chevy asked in a loud voice. "You're gay?"

"What? No!" Alyson yelled, and then she saw humor in the fact that he had thought she was a lesbian. She started laughing, and once she started, she couldn't seem to stop. It wasn't that she had a problem with how other people lived their life or their sexual orientation. She laughed because he had thought she liked women while she sat there feeling more turned on by him and his brothers than she ever had in her life.

Leaning over, she clutched her aching belly as she laughed almost hysterically. Tears rolled down her cheeks and she was gasping in air in between her uncontrollable humor.

A warm hand ran up and down her back and another rubbed her arm. She finally realized they must think she was crazy. Her hilarity slowed until only an occasional chuckle escaped, and she slowly sat up from her bent-over posture and wiped the moisture from her cheeks.

Rylan and Tarkyn, standing beside her, looked worried. Chevy was standing in front of the desk with a concerned expression on his face.

"What was that all about?" Tarkyn asked.

"I'm not gay."

"Yeah, I kinda figured."

"How did you make your eyes glow?" Alyson looked at Rylan.

"We'll get to that in a minute." Rylan took her hand and helped her from the seat. She didn't protest because she had no idea what he wanted until he sat down in the chair and pulled her onto his lap.

"Why are you afraid of men? Or is it just us in particular you're scared of?" Chevy asked.

"I'm not scared of you."

"Good." Rylan tilted her face up so he could see her eyes. "Why did Tarkyn complimenting you make you angry?"

"I already told you," she shot back.

"Not good enough. Explain!" Rylan demanded.

Why am I letting him control me? More importantly, why do I like it?

Alyson wondered why deep down inside she knew she trusted these three men not to hurt her. She'd always followed her instincts before. Her gut had gotten her out of many a tight spot when dealing with some of the violent assholes she'd had to face, but the fact that it told her to trust the Friess brothers scared her.

And then she had an epiphany. She wasn't nervous around these men because she was concerned they would hurt her, she was wary because of the way they made her feel.

She was fighting her own feelings and attraction toward them.

Chapter Four

Tarkyn watched Alyson come down from her laughing fit. That hadn't had anything to do with Chevy's question, he decided. It was like she had needed a stress outlet and once her amusement had begun, she hadn't seemed to be able to control it. Now he watched as she sobered, appearing to assess Rylan with her gaze. She visibly gathered her courage by sitting up straighter and pushing her shoulders back.

"I don't like men because they always end up hurting the ones they are supposed to love."

"Did someone hurt you?" Chevy asked with a scowl.

"No. But I have no intention of putting myself in that position."

"Why didn't you like my compliment about the way you smell?" Tarkyn asked again.

Her shoulders drooped a bit before she answered. "Because no one ever gives me compliments and you're only trying to get me into your bed."

A frown formed on her face and then her mouth opened as if in shock. "Oh. My. God. That's why you changed the delivery schedule, isn't it? You only wanted to spend time with me so you could fuck me."

Alyson pushed off Rylan's lap and headed toward the door, but Chevy moved quickly and blocked her exit.

"Get out of my way," she yelled.

Tarkyn had had enough. He knew she was nervous of them, but she needed to know that she meant more to them than a quick fuck. She was their mate, and she wouldn't be leaving until she understood what they needed from her. Alyson was an independent, sassy woman, and he liked that about her. Even though they didn't know her well, he knew he wouldn't have any trouble falling in love with her as they got to know her better. He moved quickly and scooped her up into his arms and sat on the sofa. She pushed against his chest and squirmed, trying to get away.

"Settle down, Alyson. I want you to listen to what we have to say, and then if you still want to go, you can."

She stopped struggling. "Do you promise?"

"Yes, I promise."

"We're very attracted to you, Alyson, and we want to make love with you, but we know you aren't ready for that just yet. You have to understand that there is more to what we're feeling than just attraction. We care deeply for you."

"Oh, come on. You don't even know me." Her hand landed on his shoulder, and she pushed again.

"Stop it! I haven't finished." Tarkyn shifted her in his arms and slung a thigh over hers. He wrapped an arm around her waist. Taking a deep breath, he went for broke. "We are werewolves, Alyson, and you are our mate."

She stared at him as if he were crazy. Her mouth opened and closed a few times, and then she tightened her lips into a thin line and burst out laughing again. Lowering her head against his chest, she chortled and snickered until finally she got herself under control once more.

"Yeah, and I'm Sleeping Beauty," she snorted and looked from Rylan to Chevy and back up to him.

"I'm not joking, Alyson. We are werewolves and you are our mate."

"Oh, pull the other one," she sniffed and pushed against his chest again.

"Show her." Tarkyn nodded at Chevy.

Chevy pulled his T-shirt up over his head, kicked off his shoes, and then began to remove his jeans. She glanced at his feet for a moment, looking utterly entranced at how large they were, and then her eyes traveled up the length of his body.

"What the hell are you doing?" Alyson gasped, her eyes glued to Chevy's body. She squirmed on Tarkyn's lap, her heartbeat escalating and her breath panting fast as she stared at Chevy's naked form. He smelled her arousal as it seeped from her body and couldn't contain a growl of approval from rumbling up out of his chest. "You are crazy."

"Watch Chevy, honey, and don't be scared. Just remember that we are your mates and would never do anything to hurt you. It's our job to protect you."

The outline of Chevy's body began to blur, and then he dropped down to his hands and knees on the carpeted floor. His muscles and bones contorted, and popping and cracking sounds filled the room as his brother went through the change. Tarkyn kept his eyes on Alyson, gauging her reaction to the phenomenon of their Lycan genes at work. She was clutching his arm and digging her nails into his skin as she hyperventilated. Finally Chevy was before her in wolf form, and he moved slowly toward their mate, whining quietly.

"No fucking way is this true. I have to be hallucinating. What did you put in my drink?"

"It's real, baby." Rylan sat down beside them and took one of her hands in his. "Deep down, you know what you're seeing is real. You feel the attraction, the pull toward us. I know you do, so don't you dare deny it."

"How is this even possible? There's no such thing as werewolves. It's just myth and legend," Alyson whispered, her voice sounding hoarse with emotion.

"Haven't you ever thought that some stories may have been based on fact? We were born with the Lycan gene, honey. It has been in our family for generation after generation. Only the males in our family are born shifters. In fact there are hardly ever any females born at all.

Most of us go through life hoping to meet the one true love meant for us, but not everyone is lucky enough to find their mate. We are some of the lucky ones, and there is no way we are letting you get away."

* * * *

Alyson stared at the large, golden-furred wolf with incomprehension. She had seen Chevy change from man to animal with her own eyes and still couldn't believe that what she was seeing was true. The wolf walked closer and stared at her with his glowing gold eyes. Pressing herself closer to Tarkyn, she dug her nails into Rylan's hand as nervousness permeated her body. Again, she wasn't afraid, but she was anxious and tense as she stared at what she thought was an apparition. The animal stopped within touching distance and then nudged her knee with its snout and whined again.

Without thought she released Rylan's hand and, trembling, reached out to the wolf. Another gasp escaped from between her lips as her fingers connected with his fur. A smile of awe pulled at the corners of her mouth. She hadn't expected that his coat would feel so soft and silky. Alyson had thought his fur would feel thick and coarse. She jumped and began to pull her hand away when Chevy rumbled with pleasure, but when he moaned, she sank her fingers into his coat and scratched down his back. She slid her fingers up again until she was rubbing behind his ears. He tilted his head as if giving her better access and chuffed with satisfaction.

Chevy gave her hand a lick and then backed up. His animal body blurred, and once again the horrid popping and cracking sounds echoed through the room as his body seemed to twist and contort until he was once more a man. He rose to his feet, and she couldn't stop her eyes from wandering over his buff body. The man was built and ripped and his muscles rippled as he moved, but what drew her attention was the large, engorged cock pointing straight at her. It seemed the saying about large feet was true.

Alyson held in the giggle as he dressed, and she sighed with disappointment when his clothes once more covered his sexy form. Her mind was racing at what felt like fifty million miles a minute, but she couldn't hold on to any one thought until Rylan's last words echoed through her mind over and over again.

There is no way we are letting you get away.

"Please let me up." She pushed against Tarkyn again and exhaled with relief when he let her go this time. She paced back and forth a few times in front of them, keeping her eyes on them from her peripheral vision. Chevy was once more leaning against the wall near the door and Rylan and Tarkyn were watching her from the sofa.

She stopped pacing and sat on the edge of one of the large desks. "Is a mate what I think it is?"

"It depends on what you think that term means. Why don't you tell us?" Tarkyn suggested.

"Um, the only word that comes to mind is like a—wife."

"That is exactly what being a mate means." Rylan crossed his arms over his muscular chest. "But the commitment between mates is so much more than a human wedding ceremony. If we claim you, we would all make love with you and have to bite you. The bite from a werewolf somehow transfers some of our DNA to you and we will be linked for all time. We would never, ever leave you. We wouldn't want to be without you and neither would you want to be without us. If you ever left us after we were mated, you would feel as if your heart had been ripped out. If you left us after we were mated, you would condemn us to a slow, painful death. Wolves mate for life and cannot survive without having their mate close by."

"Shit!" Alyson began to pace again. "I don't do relationships. I need some time to get my head around this. I need to go home."

"Baby, please don't leave just yet." Rylan rose to his feet and moved in front of her. "We've only touched on us being werewolves. There is so much more you need to know."

"I can't handle any more right now. I need some space. You can't keep me here against my will. I'm going home to think. I will see you all tomorrow."

Rylan gripped her shoulders and pulled her against his body. Alyson felt his erection pressing into her stomach, and more juices leaked from her pussy as her breasts swelled and her nipples puckered.

He stared deeply into her eyes as he lowered his head, and then his lips were on hers. Her gasp gave him an advantage and he slid his tongue into her mouth and tasted every inch of her. Tangling his tongue with her hesitant one, he then caressed the roof of her mouth, tickled along her cheeks, and swept his muscle over her teeth. Alyson's body went boneless as it melted from the inside out, her womb felt heavy, and her pussy ached to be filled. If she didn't have him to lean on, she would have fallen flat on her face.

Alyson had only ever been kissed once, and it had been nothing like this one. It felt like Rylan put his whole heart and soul into that meeting of their mouths, and that scared her more than anything. She was breathless when he finally withdrew his mouth from hers, but she was pleased to note he was in the same predicament. He released her and stepped back without saying anything, only standing there watching her with a puzzled expression on his face. She decided that was her cue to leave.

She lowered her head and rushed from the room. Her cheeks felt so hot that she knew she was probably as red as a tomato. Sighing with relief when she didn't hear them following her, she literally ran down the steps to the cellar, across the concrete floor, and up the ramp to her truck. Moments later she was pulling out of the parking lot and heading for home.

What the hell have I gotten myself into now!

* * * *

That went well. Chevy stared at the door Alyson had disappeared through.

"Can't we go after her?" Tarkyn pled.

"No." Rylan scrubbed a hand over his face. "We can't scare her. Our little mate is an innocent."

"What do you mean?" Chevy asked.

"Just what I said. Alyson Redding is a virgin."

"How the hell do you know that?" Tarkyn asked. "That woman has a body made for loving."

Rylan leaned against one of the desks. "She was hesitant, as if she had no idea what to do."

"We moved too fast," Chevy said grimly. "Fuck. I was afraid of that."

"No wonder she ran," Tarkyn speculated. "Although learning that werewolves are real could do a human's head in."

"Call Jerry," Rylan ordered Chevy. "We need him to check up on her and make sure she's all right."

While Tarkyn paced and Rylan brooded from one of the desks, Chevy called Jerry. The lone wolf's first words were, "What did you do this time, pup?"

Chevy explained that they'd shown themselves to Alyson. "Could you go check on her tonight? She knows you better. Maybe she'll trust you."

"I will, but at the end of the day, you're the ones who have to protect her," Jerry said.

"Give me that." Rylan grabbed the phone from Chevy. "We know we have to protect her. I want her living with us at the pack house as soon as possible."

"And you don't want her running off."

"Fuck, no!"

"Then wait. She needs time to accept what she's seen and what you've told her. I'll keep you posted."

The line clicked, and Rylan dropped the phone on the desk in irritation. "Stubborn old wolf," he grumbled. "She's our mate, not his."

"But Jerry's trustworthy. He'll find out what Alyson is scared of."

Tarkyn was still pacing. He shook his head and said, "I don't know how much more I can stand. My wolf is pushing at me hard to go and claim her."

"You think any of us find this easy?" Chevy asked. "My cock is so fucking hard I could break a glacier, but she needs more time."

Leaving the office and his brothers, Chevy paced out to the front. Cherry ducked out of the kitchen to bat her eyes at him, but Chevy brushed past her. He needed some mundane chores to help cool his raging hunger and settle his animal to a more manageable level.

After that, there was nothing for them to do but wait until Jerry called back.

If he doesn't get some answers, what then?

Chapter Five

Every time the image of Chevy changing from man to wolf flashed across her mind, Alyson pushed it aside. She couldn't deal with what she had seen and heard this afternoon. Sighing with fatigue, she finished dressing after her shower and tried to decide what to have for dinner when there was a knock on her door. Frowning because she never had visitors, she cautiously made her way to the entrance and peeked through the peep hole.

Jerry. What's he doing here?

Alyson opened the door and stepped back to admit her boss. The delicious aroma of pizza wafted to her nose as he passed her, carrying a large box.

"I thought you'd be hungry after your day and decided that I didn't want to eat alone." Jerry carried the box into the small kitchenette and placed it on the counter. "You got any beer?"

"Yeah," Alyson replied. "Let me get it."

She got them a beer each and then took out two plates and some napkins. After they loaded their plates with pizza, she led the way to her small two-seater sofa and turned the TV on then lowered the volume and turned toward Jerry. He was eying her speculatively as he took a big bite of his pizza. Alyson could see he wanted to say something to her, and she wanted to ask the real reason he was here, but she decided to wait him out. After taking a bite of her pizza, she chewed thoughtfully and watched as a frown marred his face.

"You are attracted to Rylan, Tarkyn, and Chevy Friess, aren't you?"

"What?" Alyson asked. She had heard him clearly, but she was stunned. *Why is he asking me about the Friess brothers? Does he know they're werewolves?*

"Don't play games with me, Alyson. I can smell Rylan and Tarkyn all over you."

What does he mean he can smell them on me?

"Look, Jerry, I don't know what you're talking about."

"I know they told you what they are. Chevy told me he shifted in front of you, and I can smell their scent on you. I'm a werewolf, too, Alyson. We have a great sense of smell, so don't you dare deny that you are attracted to them."

Alyson knew she probably looked stupid with her mouth hanging open as she stared at her boss. *He's a werewolf, too?* Jerry reached over and pushed her chin up, closing her gaping mouth, and smiled at her.

"Just sit there and listen to me, Alyson. You couldn't have asked for better mates. The Friess Pack is one of the biggest in the United States. The Alphas, Jonah, Mikhail, and Brock Friess, are very fair and just, and they listen to the rest of the pack instead of just making decisions without any input. This pack has been around for generations, and if you decide to accept Rylan, Tarkyn, and Chevy, they will take good care of you. Wolves mate for life, and they would give theirs to keep you safe. Those three men would love you and protect you, and you would never want for anything. Why are you scared of that?"

Alyson finally found her voice. "I'm not scared of them."

"You're sure scared of something." Keenly eying her, Jerry took another bite of pizza, chewed, and swallowed. "What are you running from, girl?"

"What makes you think I'm running from something?" Alyson mentally cursed the raised pitch of her voice.

"Oh, come on. Do you think I was born yesterday?" Jerry reached for his beer and took a swig. "I see the way you're always looking over your shoulder. I could literally smell the fear emanating off you when you first walked in to apply for the job. Now, I can sit here all night long if need be, so you'd better think about telling me what's going on."

Alyson sighed and debated whether she should tell Jerry what was going on but then decided it was probably best if she did. What would happen if Virgil Minogue found out where she was?

"I lived and worked in Phoenix. I grew up there and was quite happy after I got out of the orphanage I lived in when I was sixteen." Alyson sipped her beer. "I worked hard and paid my way through college to get my degree and was lucky enough to find employment as soon as I had finished school."

"What did you major in?"

"Social welfare. I was working for the city helping battered women and children relocate and recover from their abusive families."

Jerry sat up straighter in his chair and waited for her to continue, but she could see the tension in his body. Alyson knew just how he felt. She felt sick to her stomach now that she was talking about her problems and pushed her beer and pizza aside.

"There was a young woman who had a six-month-old baby. She came into the shelter so battered and bruised she could barely stand. I called in a doctor to check her over, and he suggested she should be in a hospital, but she adamantly refused. Mary Minogue had broken ribs and a fractured jaw, and not one inch of her body wasn't bruised." She glanced at Jerry and saw that his knuckles had turned white from gripping his beer bottle so hard. "I nearly cried when I saw her but kept it together for Mary. God, she was scared. It seemed after her husband had beat her he threatened to kill their baby. Thank the Lord her asshole husband was drunk and passed out before he could get his hands on the sweet little girl."

Alyson realized she was crying. She wiped the moisture from her cheeks. "Mary was so scared that her husband would wake up and do what he'd said that she didn't even take the time to pack herself any clothes. She always had a bag packed for her baby, so she grabbed it and ran.

"We placed her in one of the single rooms and got her clothes and constant medical care until she'd healed. It took six fucking weeks before she didn't flinch every time the doctor came to treat her and she virtually stayed imprisoned in that room the whole time she was in the shelter.

"My boss asked me to help her go through the legalities of taking out a restraining order, and although I urged her to file for a divorce she was too scared at first. Thank God she eventually found some inner strength and divorced that bastard. The details of the proceedings came out, and while Mary never tried to have him put away, the rumors were enough to ruin her wealthy, successful, and formerly well-respected husband's career." Alyson took a deep, shuddering breath and exhaled slowly as renewed anger and anguish washed over her as she remembered all Mary's pain and suffering. "Once she was free and clear of that fucker with full custody of her baby I helped find a place out of state for her to have a fresh start. We had become quite close while she was staying at the shelter, and even though I was sad to see her go, I knew it was for the best. She could have a new life away from her abusive ex and they would be safe.

"I started getting threatening e-mails at work, but they weren't directed to me, they were more of a general threat to the shelter, and they were pretty mild threats, so I just ignored them and deleted them. Then I started getting e-mails at home to my private e-mail address, and this time they threatened me personally. I knew almost from the first that it was Mary's ex sending them. I don't know how that fucker found out Mary had stayed with us or that I was her caseworker, but he did. He wanted to find his wife and baby, but there was no way I was giving him information on his family. That asshole only wanted to hurt them more, and I wasn't about to let that happen. Not when I had just helped them escape. His e-mails terrified me."

"Why didn't you call the police?" Jerry asked. "Hell, why didn't you go to the shelter you worked for? Someone there could have protected you."

"Mary's husband was a very influential man and well connected, and he felt that I somehow convinced Mary to divorce him and in doing so ruined his life and career. He threatened me by saying he was going to pay some women he knew to go to the police and tell them they were mistreated by someone at the shelter and then use his connections to shut it down. I couldn't risk that happening.

"So many women and children went there looking for help and protection when they had nowhere else to go. There was no way I was going to hang around and watch him destroy so many more lives." Alyson sighed. "I didn't want to be the deciding factor in that asshole hurting more people.

"Besides, I knew that Mary was safely hidden. If he couldn't get to me, then he couldn't get to Mary either. Even a man with Virgil Minogue's resources could only find her with a lot of effort. I packed up my stuff, handed in my resignation, and worked my way to Aztec. It took me six months to get here. I didn't want to make it easy for that asshole if he was following me. I was careful and spent most of the time looking over my shoulder." Alyson glanced at Jerry and shrugged. "You know the rest."

"You can't stay here by yourself. It's not safe." Jerry stood up and pulled his cell phone from his pocket. "Why don't you start packing while I call in reinforcements?"

"What are you talking about?" Alyson asked as she, too, rose from the sofa. "I'm safe enough. Virgil doesn't know where I am."

"Are you sure about that?" Jerry spun and pinned her with a frown. "You've been traveling under your real name. When you filled out paperwork to work for me, you used your social security number, and this isn't the first job you've had since leaving home. Employers, me included, have run background checks on you and paychecks have been deposited into your bank account every step of the way. A clever man or a rich one could use any of those to find out where you are."

Alyson felt the blood drain from her face. *Shit! How could I be so naïve?* Virgil probably knew where she was every step of the way. It didn't take a genius to realize it would be easy to find someone from their social security number, especially if he had help, like a private investigator. Even though Virgil had been a drunk and abusive, he wasn't short on funds. He'd been a hedge fund manager, and Mary had told her his parents had been wealthy and powerful and had left him with a large amount of cash after they had died.

"Rylan," Jerry said into his phone. Alyson moved closer and shook her head. Why was he calling the Friess brothers? She could take care of herself. She had been doing it for a long time.

Jerry scowled at her but continued with his conversation. "You need to get over to Alyson's right now. She needs to be kept safe. I'll explain everything when you get here."

Alyson frowned as Jerry rattled off her address and then disconnected the call. "What the hell did you call him for?"

"You remind me of my niece, girl. Do you think I'll just sit around and do nothing when you're in trouble?" Jerry asked gruffly. "Go and start packing, because you aren't going to have a choice when Rylan gets here."

"You can't tell me what to do!" Alyson yelled and then took a deep breath as she tried to control her frustration. "I am an adult, for goodness' sake."

She picked up the half-eaten pizza and carried her plate to the kitchen, where she dumped the pizza in the trash and then filled the sink with hot, soapy water. The kitchen was so small she didn't have the luxury of a dishwasher. A noise behind her alerted her that Jerry had followed her.

"If you don't want all your stuff packed haphazardly, I would start getting busy if I were you."

"I'm not leaving. You and those furry butts can't make me do anything I don't want to. I think you should leave."

"Oh, no. I'm not going anywhere. I know I've only known you for two weeks, Alyson, but you are like a niece to me and I'm not going to stand by and watch you get hurt."

Alyson spun around to face Jerry and slammed her hands on her hips, heedless that they were dripping and soapy.

"Look, I really appreciate it that you are looking after me, Jerry. I really do, but I have been taking care of myself for years. I don't need your or their help."

"God, you sound like you've lived for fifty years instead of only twenty-three. I understand you don't want to lose your independence, Alyson. Just give those men a chance. You have no idea what you would be throwing away. Don't live with regret for the rest of your life because you're afraid. I had the chance to be happy, and I let my fear dictate my decisions. I have regretted that for years. Don't end up bitter and lonely like I have because you're fearful."

Alyson hated to see sadness and loneliness in her gruff boss's eyes. He'd touched her heart by telling her she was like a niece to him. She opened her mouth to reply, but a knock on the door halted her speech. She glanced nervously at the door but didn't move toward it. Jerry gave her a last look and then went to answer the knock.

Rylan walked across the threshold of her small house with Tarkyn and Chevy following right behind. Her breathing escalated as their imposing presence seemed to suck the oxygen out of the room. God, they were magnificent. Her breasts swelled and her nipples turned turgid. Alyson squeezed her thighs together, trying to ease the ache in her clit and pussy as fluid seeped out onto her panties.

"What's going on, Jerry?" Rylan hadn't taken his eyes off her from the moment he walked into her small house, and although she tried to break their connection, she couldn't seem to manage it.

Jerry began to explain, which pissed her off, but Alyson couldn't find her voice, so she turned her stare into a scowl and narrowed her eyes.

Tarkyn and Chevy walked around Rylan and skirted Jerry until they were standing next to her in the kitchen. She wanted to rush to her bedroom and lock herself in, but she was frozen in place. When they each placed a hand on her back, she came out of her trance and tried to move away. Before she had taken three steps, Tarkyn snagged her around the waist and pulled her back against his front. She inhaled deeply when she felt the hard ridge of his erect cock against the top of her ass and the small of her back. The guy was huge.

"Pack your stuff, Alyson. You're coming home with us," Rylan said in a voice steely with determination.

"I'll leave you to it," Jerry said as he scooped the truck keys up from the counter and moved toward the door. "Don't worry about the truck, honey. I'll get one of the others to pick it up tomorrow."

"What do you mean you'll have someone pick the truck up?"

"It's too dangerous for you to be making deliveries alone. You can come back to work when all this is over." Just before he closed the door he looked around Rylan at her. "Just remember what I said, Alyson, and call me if you want to talk."

Alyson pulled away from Tarkyn and eyed Rylan warily as she moved toward the sofa. *Shit, what am I going to do now?* If Jerry wasn't going to let her work until she was safe, there was no way she was going to be able to pay her bills. *God save me from overbearing men!* They could demand all they wanted, but there was no way she was going home with them. She would just have to find another place of employment, but with the economic downturn and high unemployment rates, that wasn't going to be so easy. She sat down and stubbornly crossed her arms over her chest, staring at the TV, pointedly ignoring them.

"Okay, if that's the way you want to play it, you just sit there and rest." Rylan walked into her bedroom.

Alyson shot off the sofa and hurried after him.

"Just what the hell do you think you're doing? Get out! I don't want you here." She glared at him and pointed toward her front door.

"You can protest all you want, but I know you want us just as much as we want you. I can smell you creaming from here."

"I can't help the way my body responds to you. Shit." Alyson turned away from him and began pacing the small space between her TV and sofa. "I can't believe you three. I don't need or want your help. Please just leave."

Alyson made her way back to the sofa and threw herself on it in a fit of pique. Tarkyn came over and knelt at her feet while Chevy took the seat next to her. She was surrounded by their heat and masculine scents, which caused her pussy to contract and gush out more fluid. Rylan stood in the doorway of her small bedroom, watching her.

"Aly, we can't leave you here alone when you're in danger." Chevy placed his hand on her knee. "We are your mates and it's our job to protect you. We want you in our lives, honey, but we aren't going to force you to do anything you don't want to. My brothers and I share a suite of rooms in the pack house, and we have a spare bedroom you can use. You can have it all to yourself. We promise not to invade your privacy."

That didn't sound as bad as she'd thought. Considering how bossy they were, it almost seemed reasonable. But she stood firm. "I don't need your protection."

Rylan moved closer and stood over her but then he leaned down so he could see her eyes. "You do need protection. That asshole probably already knows where you live and is biding his time to come after you. He could even have hired someone else to do his dirty work for him. Are you willing to let him torture you until he has the information he needs? You are the only person who knows what his wife and baby's new names are and where they've gone, Alyson. He isn't going to let up until he has what he wants."

They're right. And they would protect me…No. Be firm. "I can look after myself."

"You are so fucking stubborn," Tarkyn snapped and gripped her upper arms. His hold was firm but caused her no pain. He moved in closer until their noses were nearly touching. "Are you invincible, Alyson? Can you face a bullet and not get hurt? He is going to come after you and do whatever his sick mind can think up and cause you pain without a qualm. Don't you get that?"

"Of course I do. I'm not stupid," she cried out.

"Then why are you acting it?" Rylan squatted at her side. "You've already seen the damage that bastard can do. Do you think he's just going to walk up to you and ask you politely where his wife and daughter are?"

Alyson shook her head. She knew what they were saying was true. Virgil Minogue had threatened to beat and rape and then kill her if she didn't tell him where Mary and their daughter were. But Alyson was determined not to give him anything on his family. She would take all the information on them to the grave with her if she had to.

"Darlin'." Chevy rubbed her arm. "Please let us help you. No one should have to face what you're facing without help. Please?"

Alyson sighed and closed her eyes. They were getting to her, but although she was scared out of her wits that Virgil would find her, what she felt for the three Friess brothers scared her more. It wasn't because she was beginning to care for them. She refused to entertain the thought. It was because she had seen how lost the shelter's women and children had been after things had gone bad. Not all the women she had helped had been from abusive relationships. Some of them had found themselves without a home and had come seeking help at the shelter until they had gotten over the shock of finding themselves adrift after sharing their lives with someone they had thought of as special. What those bewildered women had needed was a shoulder to cry on and for someone to listen to them. Then, after they had expelled their hurt, anger had taken over. Many times Alyson had watched the women gather themselves, determined to turn their lives around and start over.

Alyson didn't want to suffer through what those poor women had. The pain and devastation she had seen in their eyes had been heartbreaking. She had vowed never to get mixed up with a man, ever.

She opened her eyes to find Chevy's mouth close to hers. She licked her lips and stared at his. He leaned forward and brushed his warm, soft flesh back and forth over hers, like he was easing her into accepting his mouth. He sucked her lower lip between his and nibbled on it lightly with his teeth.

Alyson moaned and pressed her body into his until her cotton-covered nipples were rubbing against his chest. Chevy released her lip, opened his mouth over hers, and thrust his tongue into her depths. He tasted so good. His spicy, masculine flavor exploded on her taste buds, and she responded by tangling her tongue with his. All her previous resolutions faded. She knew she would never get enough of him and his brothers.

Chevy wrapped his arms around her, pulled her onto his lap, and deepened the kiss even more. Alyson hadn't known such feelings or desires existed until she'd met these three men. Her blood heated from the inside and her pussy clenched and released with each swipe of his tongue over hers. He kissed her with such hunger that her body went up in flames.

A hand cupped her breast and flicked her nipple. Another hand molded her other breast and pinched her aching peak between thumb and finger. It was enough to send her hurtling over the edge and into paroxysms of pleasure. Her cry of rapture was muffled by his mouth, and the hands on her breast pulled at her nipples until the last shudder left her body.

When Chevy withdrew his mouth from hers, she was pleased to find he was panting as heavily as she was.

"You are so fucking sexy, baby," Rylan whispered in her ear and then nipped her earlobe. "You look beautiful when you come."

Alyson turned to look at Rylan and Tarkyn as more heat rushed into her cheeks. She had been so wrapped up in Chevy she had almost forgotten his brothers were there.

You're lying, girl. You knew they were there the whole time, and they helped you get off without even taking your clothes off.

Shut up, Alyson told her inner voice.

Though she could deny it all she wanted, she knew that she would go home with them. At least she would have the protection they'd offered, she thought, but she didn't fool herself that that was the only reason she was going along with them.

Oh God, Alyson, you are so screwed.

Chapter Six

Rylan nipped and licked Alyson's earlobe and then placed his nose against the skin of her neck and inhaled deeply. His wolf was clamoring for dominance, telling him to claim his mate by biting the tender place where her neck and shoulder met. He let a growl rumble up from his chest as he fought for supremacy. Biting Alyson there would claim her as his. His wolf didn't want to wait until she was ready, but Rylan would never allow himself to claim her without her permission. His human side won, but his mate had stiffened at his growl.

The tension seeped from his muscles when he didn't smell fear on her. She was nervous but not frightened. That was something at least. Taking a deep breath, he pulled back and slowly rose to his feet. The pressure his jeans had been placing on his hard, aching cock eased slightly as he straightened.

He held a hand out toward her. "Come and help me pack your stuff, baby. You don't want me to do it all if you don't want your clothes all wrinkled."

Rylan's tension eased even more when she placed her hand in his and let him help her up. Then he looked at his brothers. "Why don't you two start packing up the kitchen?"

"Oh. No, wait. You don't have to do that," Alyson said over her shoulder as he started to pull her toward the bedroom.

"We want to help you, Alyson," Chevy said.

"What I meant was that everything in here stays. The only belongings I have are in my bedroom and the bathroom. The place was fully stocked, including crockery, silverware, and linen."

"All the better." Tarkyn grabbed the plate on the coffee table and the empty pizza box. "Chevy and I will clean up while you and Rylan gather your things."

Rylan let go of Alyson's hand and began to open drawers, pulling her things out and placing them on the bed. "Do you have a suitcase, baby?"

"Yeah, I have two. They're on the top shelf in the closet. I'll go and get my things from the bathroom."

Rylan slid the door to her closet open and silently cursed when he saw how little she had. The dresser had only been half full, and she only had three bras. At least Alyson had more pairs of panties. He pulled the cases down and tried to fold her things carefully and put them in the case. Rylan had managed to fold her only two sweaters before she was back from the bathroom. She had a small clear plastic bag containing the bare necessities like generic shampoo and conditioner as well as deodorant, toothpaste, a toothbrush, and stuff all females needed. What pissed him off was that she had nothing to pamper herself with. There were no moisturizers or creams. He bit his tongue and kept quiet as he pulled a pair of jeans off the hanger.

"Here, let me do that." Alyson smiled at him as she placed the impromptu toiletry bag into one of the cases.

Curiosity got the better of him. "Is this all you have?"

As soon as he asked, he mentally cursed his own bluntness. Red tinged her cheeks, and he felt like a real bastard. "I'm sorry, baby. I didn't mean to embarrass you. I just thought you would have more. I thought since you had a degree you would have had some savings from your previous job."

"I did." She whispered her reply and lowered her head as she pulled her lower lip into her mouth. "I couldn't stand to see the disappointment on the faces of the kids when we let them go through the secondhand clothes that were donated."

"You used your own money to buy them new stuff?" Rylan asked as he dropped the jeans onto the bed and pulled her into his arms.

"They looked so sad, lonely and dejected. I just wanted to make them smile, to give them something nice for once in their lives."

Rylan wrapped his arms around her waist, pulled her in tight against his body, and kissed the top of her head. "You are such an amazing woman. You are going to fit in so well with the other women."

Alyson pulled away with a jerk and asked shrilly, "You have other women?"

"No! Fuck, Alyson. I can't believe you asked that." He gripped her shoulders so she couldn't back any further away from him. "We live in a very large house with all our relatives. The other women are mated to our cousins. Michelle is our queen and mated to our Alphas, Jonah, Mikhail, and Brock Friess. The Alphas are our leaders. Then there is Keira, who is mated to Jake, Greg, and Devon Domain. Talia is mated to Blayk, Chris, and James Friess, and Samantha is mated to Justin, Roan, and Chet Domain. And lastly, Rochelle is mated with Jarrod, Malcolm, and Braxton Friess. Angela is our cook and housekeeper, and her daughter Cindy helps her with everything."

"Wow, you have a big family." Alyson sighed, and to him it sounded almost wistful.

"Yes, we do, and the people I mentioned are only the ones already mated."

"You mean there are more of you?"

"There sure are, baby. There are a lot of single wolves I haven't mentioned yet. But don't worry. You'll learn everyone's names eventually. Wolves like to be in a pack. We all live and work together. It just makes it easier with all the businesses we run."

When she pulled back, Rylan released her, and she continued to fill her cases with her things. Since she didn't have much, it took her no time at all. She started to pick up her suitcase after closing it but didn't get the chance.

"Let me take that, honey." Tarkyn took the case from her hand and then grabbed the other one off the bed.

"The kitchen is spic and span, and I've dusted the living room," Chevy said as he sauntered into Alyson's room. "Is this it?"

"Yeah. Why don't you carry Alyson's bags out to the truck while we do one last check through?" Rylan suggested, and Chevy took the bags from Tarkyn, and then Rylan spoke to his brothers through their mind link. *"The first chance we get, we are taking our mate shopping and buying her a whole new wardrobe."* Then he went on to explain Alyson had spent her money on the kids who went through the shelter, which was why she had nothing herself.

"We can take her shopping in a couple of days," Tarkyn said. *"Let's get her settled into the den first before we go pushing her too hard. She is going to balk about us spending money on her."*

Rylan turned his head to see Alyson frowning at him. "What's the matter, Alyson?"

"You were standing there staring into space. Are you all right?"

"I'm fine, baby. I was just talking to Tarkyn." He smiled at Alyson, pleased to know she cared enough about him to be concerned for him. "Werewolves can speak to each other using their minds. We have a common pack link which enables us to communicate with all the other wolves, and each family unit has a private link they can communicate with."

"You mean like…telepathy?" Alyson asked.

"Yep," Rylan answered as he guided her from her bedroom toward the front door. "Exactly."

"That must be pretty remarkable."

"Yeah, I suppose it is." He brought her hand up to his mouth and kissed the back of it. "If you eventually agree to mate with us, we'll be able to speak to you the same way."

Rylan could have cursed when Alyson attempted to pull her hand away, and she tried to wipe all expression from her face. The last thing he wanted to do was frighten her, but it seemed he had done just that with his talk about their telepathy. Maybe she thought he would be able to read her mind. He made a note to explain he and his brothers wouldn't be able to invade her privacy in such a way.

"Please don't be afraid of us, Aly. We would never force you to do anything you don't want."

She stared back at him as if trying to see if he was being sincere while she frowned at him. The creases between her eyebrows finally eased, and she gave him a tentative smile.

"Look, I don't know you well enough to make any decisions as yet. Just be thankful I'm letting you ride roughshod over me in making me come and live in your spare room."

Rylan didn't like what she'd said. "You wouldn't be coming to our den unless you wanted to, Alyson, so please don't insult my integrity by lying to yourself and me."

Alyson pulled her hand from his and looked around her small living quarters before lifting her gaze to his eyes. She drew in a deep, ragged breath and then exhaled slowly. "You're right. I'm sorry. I didn't even realize I was fooling myself." Reaching out, she placed her hand on his arm. "Why am I so drawn to you and your brothers?"

Rylan placed his hand over hers, offering comfort. "It's because we are your mates. The physical attraction is so much more than what a human experiences."

"Okay, I can understand that, but it's not enough for me, Rylan. I need more than just attraction."

Rylan pulled her into his arms and rested his head on top of hers. She felt so damn right in his arms. He hoped she would be comfortable with them soon. Not only was the wolf in him clamoring to claim its mate, but so was the man.

"I know you need more time, baby. Our feelings will develop more deeply as we get to know each other. We are meant to be together. All of us. You can deny it as much as you want to, but you know what I'm saying is true."

"Are we ready to go?" Chevy asked as he entered the small house after loading the last of Alyson's stuff into the truck.

"I have to let my landlord know I'm leaving. The elderly couple in the main house are nice people. It would be rude if I just up and left without a word."

"I've already taken care of it, honey," Tarkyn said as he, too, reentered her temporary home. "The owners didn't mind voiding the lease after I explained that you'd be moving in with someone else." Rylan saw the flash of fire in her eyes and knew his brother was about to get it.

Alyson pulled out of his arms and walked toward Tarkyn until her toes were nearly touching his. "You arrogant asshole. You had no right to do that. This place was leased in my name, and it was my responsibility to take care of the necessary arrangements."

Tarkyn smirked at her and then leaned down until his forehead was touching Alyson's. "I am one of your mates, and as such, it is my duty to help you and see that you are safe. Don't get sassy with me, little girl. I was just trying to help you."

Alyson was panting with ire, but she didn't answer Tarkyn back. Rylan wondered if she was at a loss for words or if maybe she was starting to accept that she truly wasn't alone anymore. He hoped it was the latter. She just continued to glare at Tarkyn, and Rylan could see his brother struggling as she unconsciously challenged him. His eyes changed to gold and began to glow. Alyson stepped back quickly with a gasp, but even as she backed up, she never removed her gaze from his brother.

Rylan moved in close until his front was touching her back and placed his hands on her hips to keep her still. "Are you scared, baby?" He inhaled deeply, but still he didn't scent fear, only nervousness. "You need to learn not to confront a wolf, Alyson. If you continue to provoke a dominant animal, you may bite off more than you can chew."

Alyson threw up her hands and spun around. "See, I knew I shouldn't have agreed to come with you. You guys are going to be dictatorial, and I am not a submissive woman. This is never going to work."

"Oh, it will work, honey," Tarkyn whispered close to her ear, but Rylan could still hear his brother easily because of his wolf senses. "We don't want a submissive woman. We like you just the way you are." Tarkyn licked her neck and then nipped her earlobe, drawing a gasp from Alyson.

"Come on, let's get out of here." Rylan wrapped his arm around Alyson's waist when Tarkyn backed off, and he turned her toward the door. She picked up her purse and the key, but he took the key from her hand and locked up before sliding the key back under the door.

Chevy was waiting at the door to their truck, ready to help her in, but she just shook her head and dug in her purse. She backed away and then crossed the road to a small car which had definitely seen better days. If Rylan had his way, the vehicle she drove would be sent to the scrap heap, but he would have to wait to gain her trust before he made such a decision.

"Chevy, go with Alyson," Rylan ordered.

Alyson was in the process of getting in her car. She pulled her seat belt on and then looked over to him through the open window. "I'm quite capable of driving on my own. I can just follow you to your house."

"You're not driving by yourself. Chevy is going with you," he stated firmly.

Alyson muttered again about "arrogant, bossy men," but he ignored her this time.

Chevy hopped in the passenger seat, and Rylan watched Alyson pull her car out onto the street.

He stood and watched them go.

"What's up?" Tarkyn asked.

"She has to learn that when we say something, we mean it."

Tarkyn was wearing a goofy smile. "She likes that we're arrogant and bossy. She just won't admit it."

Rylan hoped that was true, but he wasn't sure. "And the Alphas? They're a hell of a lot bossier than we are. If she challenges them, can we protect her?"

"You're worrying about nothing. The Alphas are lenient when it comes to women. The females of our pack are to be cherished and protected. Especially since Alyson doesn't know the ropes yet."

Rylan shook his head. He knew Alyson would fit in fine with the other women of the pack. They, too, were feisty and independent. But it would be just like her to go head to head with Jonah, not realizing what it meant to challenge an Alpha wolf. *She won't like the taste of Pack Law.*

Tarkyn slapped him on the shoulder and drew him from his thoughts. "Let's catch up. Don't want them to start the party without us."

"No, we don't." Rylan unlocked their SUV and pulled out toward the pack house.

Let's see if she is as accepting of the rest of us as we've been of her.

Chapter Seven

Alyson listened as the three Friess brothers debated about ways to bring more business to the Aztec Club. She had already learned that Rylan was a bit of a hard ass and Tarkyn could be just as bad. Chevy seemed to be the mediator and thinker even though he was the youngest of the three.

"I think we should bring in live bands," Rylan said in a firm voice.

"Wasn't that Cherry's suggestion?" Tarkyn asked critically. "She just wants a chance to schmooze with musicians."

"I know she's not the sharpest knife in the drawer, but she's allowed to have a good idea occasionally. The more people we can get to visit our town, the better our profits will be and the more we can do for the local economy."

"Rylan, we already have too many humans living here," Tarkyn responded. "The pack members have to be cautious enough. I think bringing in even more of them will be a mistake. We only have a few women, and we don't want them to be in danger from strangers."

"Guys, stop!" Chevy butted in. "You are both right. Bringing in live music will benefit all of us, and, Tarkyn, you know damn well that if any of our women were in trouble, our pack members would step in to protect them. Besides, do you really think that their mates will let them visit the club without them? Get real."

Alyson was intrigued by how they hashed out their decisions. She wondered if Rylan ever put his foot down, making an idea stick whether the other two agreed or not. She wouldn't put it past him.

"Are you all right, Alyson? You've been quiet ever since we got back home."

Alyson was fine other than feeling very overwhelmed. The large automatic wrought-iron security gates had only been a prelude to what she was seeing at the house. Of course she had realized that the place would be massive since the men had told her that their family was large and they lived as well as worked together. But at the sight of the house, her breath had caught in her throat, and not until pinpricks of light formed before her eyes did she start to breathe again. The place was as big as a palace. She was just thankful they had taken her up to the second story and straight to their suite of rooms. Alyson wasn't sure she could have dealt with meeting more werewolves right at that moment.

She was currently sitting on a large leather sofa with Chevy seated next to her while Rylan and Tarkyn sat in armchairs as they continued throwing ideas at each other.

"Yeah." She cleared her croaky throat. "I'm fine." Her stomach chose that moment to rumble hungrily. The two bites of pizza she'd consumed hadn't been anywhere near enough to satisfy her. Given all that had happened tonight, she should have been too shocked to eat, but it seemed her body was going to continue to complain until it was appeased.

Chevy stood up and held his hand out to her. "You're hungry. Come on and I'll take you down to get something to eat."

"I can wait until morning." Alyson eyed his hand and then realized that Rylan and Tarkyn were no longer speaking. "It's getting late. I don't want to be a bother."

Chevy took her hand in his and helped her up. "You could never be a bother, darlin'. Angie always leaves sandwiches in the fridge in case someone gets hungry."

Alyson looked around as Chevy led her out of their rooms and down the long corridor. The carpet was expensive and luxurious. She felt like she sank about an inch as she walked over the plush cushioning. The walls were painted a nice neutral beige color and the stairs' handrails were a deep polished mahogany. She felt a little out of place because she could tell these people had money. Although the quality was the best, the massive house wasn't ostentatious.

Chevy guided her down the stairs and into the kitchen on the right of the hall. Her sneakers squeaked as she walked over the highly polished tile floor. She heard voices as she entered and the conversation stopped as she walked beside Chevy further into the room. On one side of the massive room was a large gourmet kitchen that would be a chef's dream, separated by a large granite counter. On the other was the dining area, outfitted with a shiny wood table large enough to seat at least fifty people. Sitting at the head of the table were three very tall, handsome, muscular men and a pretty woman with a toddler on her lap. Alyson froze and lowered her head, feeling like an intruder.

"Alyson, these are the Alphas of our pack, Jonah, Mikhail, and Brock. This is their mate, Michelle, and their son, Stefan. Alphas, this is Alyson Redding, our mate."

"Hi, Alyson," Michelle said with a smile toward her. "Welcome to the pack house. If you have any questions or just need someone to talk to, please don't hesitate to come find me."

"Hi," Alyson replied. "And thank you." She watched Michelle play with her son. She could see the woman and her mates doted on him. He was a happy and very healthy little boy. Giving a wistful sigh at what she had missed out on as a child, she pushed her thoughts aside and turned to Chevy.

"Why don't you go and sit with Michelle while I get you some food, darlin'?"

At first Alyson felt a bit awkward, but the more she spoke to Michelle and her mates and played with little Stefan, the more relaxed she felt. Just as she finished eating her sandwich, Rylan and Tarkyn came into the dining room with three other men and another woman.

Rylan sat next to her and introduced her to Jarrod, Malcolm, and Braxton Friess and their mate, Rochelle. He told her that Jarrod was the town sheriff and his brothers were his deputies. Then, to Alyson's irritation, Rylan told them about her previous job and the threatening e-mails she had been getting.

"Jarrod, I want you to find out everything you can about Virgil Minogue."

"Sure. I'll look into it first thing."

"Look, I don't think…" Alyson ground her teeth when Rylan continued talking over the top of her.

"That bastard probably knows where Alyson is and has just been biding his time. I want to know where that fucker is if at all possible."

"I said I'll look into it, Rylan." Jarrod sounded a bit annoyed with Rylan, and he wasn't the only one.

She understood he was trying to help her and keep her safe, but to talk about her and her problems like she wasn't even in the room pissed her off to no end.

She pushed her chair back angrily, leaned over, and placed her palms down on the tabletop. "That's enough. I'm sitting right here and you are talking about me as if I'm not even in the room. How rude can you get?"

"You go, girl," Michelle said loudly and smiled at her.

Alyson had forgotten she and her husbands were also in the room, and even though she knew they were the leaders of this band of people, she didn't give a shit. There was no way she was letting Rylan take over her life.

"Sit down, Alyson," Rylan demanded.

"No, I won't." She glared at Rylan and then slowly straightened when his eyes turned gold and he growled at her. Carefully skirting the chair, she edged away from the table toward the door. *Maybe it wasn't such a good idea to come here after all.*

"Uh, Alyson, can you please come here for a moment?" Michelle asked hesitantly.

"Stay out of this, mate," Jonah said in a growly voice.

"Oh, bite me," Michelle replied.

Alyson wasn't sure if Michelle should have said that to the pack leader and bit her lip as she waited to see what he would do to her. *Will he hit her?*

"With pleasure, honey, but let's wait until we're alone."

"You are so bad." Michelle giggled.

"Yeah, but you like it when I'm bad."

Alyson released the tension she hadn't realized she had been holding as she watched the lovers interact, but then her muscles tautened again when she caught movement in her peripheral vision. Rylan was standing virtually on top of her and glaring at her, but it was a relief to see that his eyes were now back to their normal color. He gripped her wrist firmly but without hurting her and began to pull her from the room.

"Hey, let go." She pulled, trying to get him to release her. When he just kept going, she stuck her leg between his and tripped him.

Rylan let her go as he stumbled then spun around after he had gained his balance again. She stared at him in fascinated horror as he stalked toward her, his eyes narrowed to mere slits and his jaw clenched tight. Alyson backed up, knowing she had gone too far, and even though she regretted her actions, she was determined not to apologize or back down.

He moved so fast he was a blur, and then she squealed as her world turned upside down. He slung her over his shoulder and took off at a fast clip. The floor whirled by, and she realized she was in deep shit. Not willing to give in to him without a fight, she pummeled her fists against his back and bucked, careless that his broad, muscular shoulder dug into her stomach. A hard slap landed on her ass, and she screeched with excited fury. She knew deep down that Rylan or his brothers would never hurt her. Her pussy clenched and more juices leaked out onto her panties. *What is it about these men that gets me so excited?* But she wasn't about to let him or his brothers know how much they affected her. She was worried that if she gave in to her desire for them, she would be lost. She wasn't about to let that happen. Alyson went wild, cursing and screaming, trying to get him to release her.

"Put me down right now, you fucking asshole. I am not letting you hurt me."

Another hard smack landed on her bottom, making her cry out at the sting, and she renewed her efforts to get away. Her breasts were swollen and her nipples peaked as if they were begging to be touched. The deep-seated need she felt for Rylan, Tarkyn, and Chevy scared the crap out of her. She'd never experienced such internal fire or desire in her life. Just as she decided to take a bite out of his ass, she went flying through the air. Alyson screamed out with fear, but that noise was cut off as she landed on a soft surface and bounced a couple of times.

After a quick glance she realized that she was in one of their suite's bedrooms. *How the hell did he get me here so fast?* Those thoughts left her head as she looked at Rylan. He was furious. She could see the heat from his rage emanating from him. The muscles of his biceps bulged and his hands were clenched into tight fists. His body was pumped and ready to fight.

Alyson backed away from him, crab walking up the bed on her hands and feet, and whimpered when her back hit the headboard. She was trapped and had nowhere to go. Tarkyn and Chevy stood just inside the doorway of the room, their eyes going from Rylan to her and back again. Even though Rylan looked so pissed off, she still wasn't scared that he would hurt her. She was frightened of her own reaction to all three of them. The way they all looked at her made her feel sexy and feminine. Her arousal ratcheted up another notch and the itch to have them touching her was so needy her whole body felt like it was one massive ache of desire. Tarkyn looked just as angry as his older brother, but Chevy was frowning with concern.

"Don't you dare back away from me, you little hellcat. I would never hurt you," Rylan snarled at her.

"You already did," she gasped between pants and then mentally cringed because she knew that wasn't really true.

She recoiled as he moved around the end of the bed. He came closer to her, and then, to her surprise, he sat down on the side of the bed and just watched her. He took a few deep breaths and the tension slowly eased from his body. Alyson lowered her head in relief. It seemed that not all men took their anger out on women after all.

"Alyson, I would never, ever raise a hand to you. Please don't be afraid of me. I spanked your ass, baby. I didn't hit you." Rylan reached out his hand, palm up, looking her in the eye as he waited.

Alyson's apprehension slowly faded, and she reached out to place her hand in his. He turned his hand around until their fingers were threaded together.

"Baby, I know you are an independent woman and are used to taking care of yourself. I get that." Rylan gave her a slight tug and then wrapped an arm around her waist and pulled her onto his lap. "But you have to realize it is our job as your mates to make sure you are protected at all times. You also don't know that what you did just challenged my authority over you in front of my Alphas as well as other members of my pack. You have to remember that we aren't human, Alyson. If you challenge a wolf, there are consequences."

Alyson thought about all the documentaries she had seen on the TV regarding wild animals. She had recently watched a show on wild wolves, and when one of the lower pack members had challenged the alpha male over a meal, the alpha had bitten the other wolf and chased it off. She hadn't even thought about what she was doing when she had stood up for herself. No wonder Rylan had been so angry. To do so in front of the other pack members and Alphas was just asking for trouble.

"I'm sorry." Without thinking about what she was doing she stroked a hand over his pecs and lowered her eyes. "I didn't mean to goad your animal, but you made me so damn mad when you were talking about me as if I wasn't there."

"I'm sorry, too, baby. I shouldn't have done that. I should have included you in the conversation."

A tug to her hair brought her head back up. The small bite of pain went straight to her pussy, causing fluid to leak out onto her panties and her nipples to ache. She shifted on his lap. The hard muscles of his thighs flexing beneath her ass only seemed to inflame her desire to a higher level.

A low sound rumbled up out of Rylan's chest and she felt the vibrations beneath the palm of her hand. He leaned down and sniffed against her neck.

"You smell so fucking good. I want to make love with you."

Alyson squeezed her legs together, trying to relieve the ache between her thighs and stem the constant flow of juices weeping from her pussy. She had been drawn to Rylan and his brothers from the first time she had laid eyes on them in the club's cellar, and now she could imagine what it would be like to have three sets of hands and three mouths touching her.

Rylan had already shown her that he could control his temper, and he had vowed he would never hurt her, not physically. Emotionally, however, they could hurt her badly without even realizing.

He was waiting for her answer. All three of them were. Though she wanted to say yes, deep down she knew that if she stayed with them for any length of time, her heart would end up more seriously involved than it already was.

I trust them. But can I trust them with my heart?

Chapter Eight

Tarkyn watched as expressions flitted across the face of his mate, and he waited with bated breath for her to acknowledge Rylan's statement. When he'd smelled her nervousness as his brother had stalked her, he had wanted to scoop her up into his arms and hold her tight, reassuring her that none of them would ever hurt her. But since it had been Rylan she had backed away from, he'd let his dominant brother deal with their recalcitrant mate. Now that she'd calmed down, Tarkyn could smell her arousal. The scent was so sweet and musky it was driving him and his wolf crazy. When he glanced at her chest he could see her nipples poking against the material of her shirt, and then he noticed how hard she was squeezing her legs together. As if she was trying to scratch an itch or appease an ache.

Nah-ah. Not happening, honey. If you want someone to help relieve that ache, then we are gonna do it for you.

Tarkyn took the three steps needed and stood so close to Alyson that his knees touched hers, and since she was sitting on Rylan's lap he had effectually blocked her escape route if she decided to shy away from them. She slowly looked up, and when her gaze connected with his, he could see apprehensive acquiescence and heat all warring together in those pretty eyes.

"Yes," she finally whispered.

He and his wolf couldn't take any more.

He knelt down and rubbed his hands up and down her denim-clad thighs, getting closer and closer to that sweet-smelling pussy. Tarkyn leaned in and took her mouth with hunger. She moaned into his mouth and slid her tongue along his. Her little sounds of pleasure were music to his ears. He wanted her closer, needed her up against his body so he could feel all her curves and her heat. Tarkyn wrapped his arm around her waist and with the other hand helped her maneuver until she was facing him, still sitting on Rylan's lap. Her back pressed against his brother's front, her legs hooked over his thighs. Tarkyn felt his brother move his knees wider, opening her body to him even though she still had her clothes on.

He pressed his lips to hers. Her mouth was so sweet, he could just imagine how delectable her pussy would taste once he got his mouth on her wet, musky folds. He released her waist and slipped his hand up under the hem of her T-shirt. Alyson's skin was soft and warm and silky. One touch would never be enough. While keeping her mouth engaged with his, he slowly caressed her flesh, over her belly and up to her side, where he could feel the outline of her ribs. Drawing his mouth slightly from hers, he pulled her lower lip between his and sucked on her soft flesh. She moaned, and he felt the vibration of that sound against the palm of his hand. He wanted to hear more of those sweet hums and moved his hand the last couple of inches until he was cupping one lace-covered breast in his palm.

Tarkyn groaned when her nipple peaked and stabbed into his skin. He kneaded and molded her fleshy globe, and then he rasped his thumb back and forth over her turgid peak. She threw her head back until it thunked against Rylan's shoulder and mewled with her desire. Using his finger and thumb, he squeezed her nipple between his digits and watched as the muscles in her face went slack with heightened arousal. But he still wasn't satisfied. Tarkyn needed to feel her naked skin beneath his mouth, hands, and body.

"Help me get her clothes off."

Chevy moved in closer and reached for the hem of her shirt. Between the two of them they had her naked from the waist up in seconds, and then Tarkyn slipped the button from her jeans and lowered the zipper. Rylan lifted her hips and Chevy helped him tug her jeans and panties down her legs then quickly removed her shoes and socks when her pants caught around her ankles and drew them the rest of the way off.

Rylan inhaled raggedly at the same time Chevy moaned. Although they suspected their beautiful mate was a virgin, she had either waxed or shaved all the pubic hair from her mound. Cream glistened on the puffy lips of her labia, and her musky scent permeated the air more strongly now that she was naked. Her breasts were much fuller than he had suspected and were topped with dusky-rose areolas and hard nipples. He had large hands, and she would overflow them.

Alyson whimpered when Rylan cupped those puppies in his hands and then pulled her nipples out from her body. Tarkyn had to taste the sweet honey dripping from her pussy right now. He knelt down again and wrapped his arms around each of her thighs and pulled her forward, away from his brother's crotch. When he had her right where he wanted her and knew he wouldn't touch his brother, Tarkyn slid his hands under her body and gripped her ass. Her muscles clenched as he massaged her muscularly taut but fleshy cheeks, separating them and stretching her hole as he lowered his head.

He breathed in deeply, used his thumbs to spread her labial lips even more, and then licked from her pussy hole up to her protruding pink nub. She tasted sweet and spicy all rolled into one, and he was determined to lap up every single delicious drop her body produced. Tarkyn opened his mouth wide and licked up through her folds like a cat would lap up cream, but instead of taking short little laps, he took long, slow licks. Reaching further around her thigh with his right arm, he rimmed the entrance to her sheath with a finger. She squirmed, moaned, and thrust her hips up into his mouth.

Tarkyn began to penetrate her and slowly slid his finger into her warm, wet body. She was so tight he knew that once he got his cock inside her, he would have to use every ounce of his control to hold back an orgasm to make certain Alyson would reach climax first. But that was for a little later. Right now he wanted to send her to the stars.

As he eased his finger into her pussy up to the first knuckle, her inner walls clenched and tried to pull him in, but since he and his brothers suspected she was an innocent he was going to take his time and make sure this was as pleasurable as possible for his mate. He withdrew his finger slightly and then pushed in farther while laving her clit with the tip of his tongue. Every time he caressed that engorged bundle of nerves, the muscles in her legs and lower abdomen quivered. Tarkyn wondered if she would go wild when in the throes of climax.

He looked up when Chevy leaned down and kissed Alyson. Tarkyn groaned against her flesh when he saw the openmouthed kiss she shared with his brother. Glimpses of her tongue tangling with Chevy's had Tarkyn's cock pulsing against the closed teeth of his fly. Alyson's sob was muffled by Chevy's kiss as Rylan rolled her nipples and Tarkyn thrust his finger into her until he could reach no farther.

Her internal muscles clenched around his embedded digit, and when they released again, she covered his flesh with another gush of fresh cream. Tarkyn wanted to hear her climax. He wondered if she would continue to make those little whimpering, sobbing mewls or if she would scream the house down. He hoped it was the latter, because he wanted her so wrapped up in her pleasure that she finally let go and let her body take over. Their little mate had learned to be too cautious, and he wanted to know they had all of her trust.

Tarkyn pulled his finger out and then pumped two fingers back into her tight, pretty little cunt. He spread his digits as he removed them until the tips were just inside, and as he slid them back in, he searched for that sweet spot inside that all women had. When he found it, Alyson cried out and bucked so hard she nearly threw him off of her.

"Hold her down. I'm going to make her come," Tarkyn ordered his brothers through their mind link.

Gaining speed and depth with each move, he made sure to caress over her G-spot with every thrust. Then he stopped sliding his digits in and out of her body, curled his fingers, and wiggled them as he sucked her clit in between his lips and flickered the tip of his tongue back and forth over the bundle of nerves rapidly. Alyson's sobs turned to a high-pitched keening sound, and her cunt rippled around his fingers. Then she was screaming, her pussy clamping down and releasing on him as her climax swept over her. He sucked on her clit gently but firmly and tapped on her G-spot. Her cream gushed out, drenching her thigh and his hand as well as the carpet below. He released her clit and drank down the sweet honey pouring from her as he and his brothers held her jerking body still.

When the last spasm faded, the sound of their heavy, rasping breaths echoed through the room. Tarkyn kissed her pussy and the insides of her thighs and then slowly eased his fingers from her body. When he finally lifted his head to take in his mate's flushed face and her swollen lips and nipples, he knew he had never seen a more beautiful sight.

His wolf was so close to the surface, wanting to claim its mate, that his fingernails lengthened into claws. He closed his eyes and took deep breaths, trying to calm his inner animal so he wouldn't scare Alyson. By the time he was back in control, Alyson was staring at him with passion-glazed eyes as if he was a glass of water to quench her thirst.

Rylan rose to his feet, taking Alyson with him, turned, and placed her on the bed in the middle. He stepped back and began to remove his clothes. Tarkyn caught Chevy doing the same, so he did, too. All the time he watched their mate watching them until the three of them were standing before her totally naked, hungrily aroused, their cocks jutting from their bodies.

Chevy was the first to move. He grasped his cock and began stroking it as he moved toward the bed. Leaning over Alyson with his knee on the bed, he released his cock and gripped her hair. He bent down and took her mouth with a rapacious need. Tarkyn had never seen his brother so hungry before. The sight of his younger sibling eating their mate's mouth ramped up his own desire until he was in danger of shooting off before he even got his cock inside her.

Tarkyn got onto the bed on the other side and took one of her hard nipples into his mouth. She was sweet, like nothing he'd ever tasted before. He could spend hours devouring her pussy, her breasts, and every bit of available skin. Never had a woman felt so right. There was a peace inside him at having found her. Now they had her in their home and bed, he never wanted to let her go. She was theirs. Nothing and no one had better get in between her, him, and his brothers.

It was their purpose and honor to protect her, to love her, and to make love with her. He vowed to find out everything he could on this Virgil guy, and when he found the asshole, Tarkyn was going to rip his head from his fucking shoulders. No one threatened his mate and got away with it.

She sobbed into Chevy's mouth and arched her chest up into Tarkyn's. Pushing his thoughts aside, he sucked firmly on her turgid peak and pressed it against the roof of his mouth. As Tarkyn opened his eyes, Rylan moved up further between her splayed legs. His brother fondled her pussy, slipping his digits through her wet folds and drawing light circles around her wet clit. Alyson pulled her mouth away from Chevy's and whimpered as she gasped in air. Her face was flushed with renewed arousal, and if it hadn't been for Tarkyn and his younger brother, she would have been writhing all over the bed.

Alyson Redding was full of newly awakened passion, and they were just the men to put out her flames.

Rylan slid his arms beneath her legs so that her knees were bent in the crooks of his elbows. He slowly began to push his way into her body. Tarkyn could see how his brother held himself on a tight leash. Sweat formed on his brow and trickled down the sides of his face. Rylan's wolf showed in his eyes, and Tarkyn knew how much of a strain it was to fight the animal instinct to just plunge inside her with one thrust and bite her to make her theirs. He knew because he had been fighting his animal instincts from the moment he had scented her.

He watched her face as Rylan pushed into her. Alyson's eyes were glazed over with passion, and her pupils were so dilated he could barely see the color of her irises. Her lips were red, puffy, and full of blood from Chevy's kisses. Her cheeks, neck, and chest were tinged pink. She was so fucking sexy that he wanted to fuck her now, but he would have to wait his turn. As Rylan was the eldest and the most dominant of them, it was his brother's right to make love with their mate first.

Alyson thrust her hips up, trying to take more of Rylan's cock into her body, but he wasn't about to be swayed. He gripped her hips and held her down, slowly forging his way into her vagina with a shallow rocking motion of his hips. Tarkyn sat up beside her and looked down to where his brother and their woman were connected. His cock jerked and throbbed when he saw the delicate petals of her pussy stretching to accept Rylan's wide, hard cock into her body. His brother's dick glistened with the dew from her honey as he pulled back once more.

"You are so tight, baby. Don't move. I don't want to hurt you," Rylan said in a deep, husky, growly voice.

"More. Please? I need more."

"You're a virgin, Alyson. We need to go slow." Rylan held still a moment, panting, with his jaw clenched tight.

Alyson's eyes widened. "How did you…"

"We are your mates, honey. Do you think we wouldn't know something as important as that?" Tarkyn leaned down and kissed her. She sobbed into his mouth, and he swallowed her sweet sounds. She tasted so good, he couldn't get enough. He tangled his tongue with hers and reached out to pinch one of her nipples. As he plucked at her turgid peak, he sucked her tongue into his mouth and then nipped at her lower lip.

Finally, when he needed to take in more air, he lifted his head and gazed into her eyes. Although his brother was the one taking her virginity, making love to her for the first time, Tarkyn needed to feel connected to her, too. And not just on a physical level. He needed to be with her emotionally. He wished he could read her mind and know everything she needed and wanted. He would give it all to her in a heartbeat.

Rylan was buried all the way inside her pussy, and Tarkyn could see how her lower abs jumped and quivered as if trying to adjust to the intrusion into her body. He stroked his hand over her head and hair, offering comfort and trying to get her to relax.

"You feel so good, Aly. You are so fucking wet and tight," Rylan groaned. The muscles in his arms bulged and strained. Whether it was to hold back or because of the pleasure he was feeling, Tarkyn couldn't be sure. "Is it too much, baby? Do you want me to go on?"

Chapter Nine

"God, yes!" Alyson answered Rylan's question. *How could it be too much? I have three very sexy, hot, brawny men touching me.* Her whole body was one big ache and so hot with arousal she couldn't understand why she hadn't set the sheets on fire.

Rylan was buried in the depths of her pussy, stretching out her sensitive, wet tissue to the point of pain. But oh, how she loved the way he stretched her and made her burn. He'd taken his time with her as he breached her untried sheath. The sweat rolling down his face was a testament to his tightly reined control. Now he was waiting for her to adjust to his penetration.

There hadn't been any pain as he gained depth into her body, which surprised her, because she had heard that the first time a woman had sex would be painful. Maybe because she was so active, she had long since broken through her barrier. Or maybe it was because he had taken his time with her and not shoved inside with one thrust. Whatever the reason, she was grateful. Who wanted to feel pain when there was so much pleasure to be had?

Three sets of hands were on her skin. Tarkyn was kneading one of her breasts and occasionally pinching her nipple while the other hand was on her belly, sporadically caressing and rubbing her skin. Chevy had kissed her long and deep, and now he had one hand on her upper ribs and the other was threaded into her hair as if trying to keep her still. And Rylan was gripping her hips firmly, keeping her from bucking up. She felt totally controlled, and that only flamed the fire running through her body higher.

Alyson had never felt so full. Every sensation she experienced was new. Though she had no idea what would happen next or what new heights she might reach, she felt sexy, wanton, and almost cherished. What was it about these men that drew her? Never before had she let anyone dictate to her or take her over. But with them it felt almost necessary.

Since the first moment she had met them she'd wanted to be near them. Now that she was here in their house, she didn't want to leave. If she left, it would be like leaving her heart behind. It would be ripped out, and she would never be the same again.

She whimpered and then moaned when Rylan eased out slowly then thrust back in. The pleasure was so acute it was beyond imagining. Self-induced orgasms didn't even come close to how he made her feel as his hard cock massaged the internal walls of her pussy. She'd already had one mind-blowing orgasm when Tarkyn had eaten her out, but the experience of having her cunt filled was so much better. The emptiness inside was gone and she felt almost…complete.

With each rock of his hips Rylan gained speed until his flesh was slapping against hers. She could feel his balls hitting her anus every time their bodies connected, and that only seemed to ramp up her arousal another notch.

She clutched onto Tarkyn's and Chevy's arms, needing an anchor to hold on to as pleasure wracked her body from all sides. The blood racing through her veins with her rapid heartbeat was hot and molten. Her muscles were lax, and even though her body got tauter with each internal caress by his cock of her pussy, she didn't think she would have the strength to stand.

"Do you like how Rylan's cock feels inside you, honey?" Tarkyn breathed against her ear. Shivers wracked her spine and more goose bumps broke out over her skin.

"Yes," she moaned, drawing her answer out.

"I can't wait to feel your hot cunt wrapped around my cock."

"Fuck!" Rylan groaned. "She likes dirty talk. Her pussy just gripped me harder than a fist."

Rylan shifted higher onto his knees and took her with him. Her ass left the bed and her pelvis tilted, giving him better access to her pussy. He pressed into her again. She cried out as his cock penetrated her deeper than ever before. A slight pain joined her pleasure as the head of his hard rod bumped into her cervix.

"More. I need more." She gasped her demand.

"Don't worry, baby. I'll give you what you need." Rylan's face was a mask of fierce concentration as he pumped his hips.

Chevy leaned back down and kissed her. He licked along her lips and then thrust his tongue into her mouth while his hand molded around her breast and his thumb rasped across her nipple.

Warmth gathered in her lower belly, filling her womb with tingles and making it feel heavy as she melted even more. Her pussy rippled around his rapidly thrusting cock, the internal ache and the throbbing in her clit intensifying.

"You're close, aren't you, Alyson. I can't wait to feel your pussy clamping down on my cock. I want you to cover my dick with your honey. I want to bite you and make you mine. Will you let me claim you, baby?"

She was on the verge of a climax so big it almost scared her and would have agreed to anything right then.

She wanted to bare her throat to him, to feel his teeth sinking into the skin at her shoulder and connecting them together for all time. She wanted to be loved, cherished, and most of all, she wanted to belong.

But she was afraid.

Looking into her eyes, Rylan stilled. "What is it, baby?"

"It's a big decision," she whispered.

Still watching her, he nodded slowly. "If I mark you, you will be ours for all time. Do you understand, Alyson?"

"I understand. That's why I want to wait." Her heart believed they would never hurt her and would always protect her, but her mind hadn't yet learned to trust.

She wanted to tell them that, but Rylan still held her on the cusp of climax, and the words wouldn't come. Tarkyn stroked her cheek gently. "It's okay, honey. We respect your decision."

Rylan thrust slowly, drawing Alyson's attention back to him. The sight of his glowing golden eyes heightened her need even more. *If he would just speed up a little...*

"Do you want me to go on?"

The sound of his low, gravelly voice sent more tremors through her body, and a shiver coursed over her. She was so close, her pussy so tight, that she tried to push up against him to help send her over the edge into climax. His grasp on her tightened, and he stilled. Alyson growled with frustration, but she could tell by the determined look on his face that he wasn't about to let her take control.

"Answer me, baby!"

"Yes!" She practically screamed her reply, desperate to reach the nirvana waiting for her at the top of the crest.

"Good girl," Rylan groaned and began to thrust fast, hard, and deep.

The bliss which had begun to wane when he stopped moving came back with an even greater intensity. Tremors shook her body, her legs, her stomach. Her toes curled as bliss swamped her. She threw her head back and screamed. Her pussy clamped down so hard around his cock she could feel every ridge, vein, and throb as his dick shuttled in and out of her pussy. Her womb contracted, and her pussy gushed fluid, covering him with her juices as she spasmed and jerked, her sheath convulsing around him. He moaned loud and long as he pumped in and out of her body, his face a twisted, tortured mask of pleasure.

Tarkyn and Chevy moved aside. Rylan came down on top of her, covering her with his big, muscular body.

Alyson screamed again as another wave of rapture swept over her. His groan of completion was muffled against her skin, and she felt his cock expand and jerk as his warm cum bathed her cervix and internal walls. Pinpricks of light flashed before her closed eyelids. Her body shook and shuddered. Finally the last spasm waned until she was left feeling wrung out.

He lifted up onto his arms and lightly kissed her lips, and then he carefully rolled, their bodies still intimately joined, until they were both lying on their sides. She laid her head on his shoulder and arm as he pulled her in close against him, his hands running up and down her back, soothing her until the trembling in her body ceased. Alyson only became aware of Tarkyn's and Chevy's hands on her, stroking her, when Rylan finally kissed her forehead and pulled away, getting off the bed and walking toward the adjoining bathroom.

"Are you okay, darlin'?" Chevy rubbed her back.

Alyson thought about her answer before she replied. She felt wonderful. She'd never have known such bliss existed if she hadn't met the three Friess brothers.

Now that she'd had a taste, she wanted more. So much more. And although she wanted to make love with Chevy and Tarkyn, too, she was still a little protective of her feelings toward them. She wanted to spend the rest of her life living with them, loving with them, and growing old with them, but she was still apprehensive about opening herself up to them totally. She'd seen the effects of marriages gone wrong or abuse delivered to someone weaker. There was no way she was letting them do that to her. There was a small part of her that expected things to go wrong, and therefore she kept part of herself closed off.

When she was more comfortable with them and got to know them better, then she would think about opening herself up to them totally and possibly mating with them as their relationship progressed. But until then she vowed to bide her time.

"I'm wonderful," she finally answered.

Rylan came back into the room and lifted one of her legs. When he began to clean her with a warm, damp washcloth, she tried to push his hand away. Heat suffused her cheeks, and she stammered, "I can do that."

She sighed with relief and then closed her legs tight when he withdrew.

"I'll be back in a moment, baby." Rylan kissed her shoulder, and she heard him leave with Chevy. It crossed her mind to wonder where they were going, but then Tarkyn ran his hand over the outside of her thigh. She opened her eyes to see him smiling.

"Guess it's just you and me, honey."

* * * *

In the hall, where they would be safely out of earshot, Rylan turned to Chevy. "What is it?"

Chevy had told him through their mental link that they needed to have a word privately, but he'd refused to elaborate. There was nothing Chevy could say aloud that couldn't be said telepathically, so Rylan couldn't guess why they were here.

Chevy prodded Rylan in the chest. "I thought we agreed not to push her." Chevy kept his voice down, but his tone was urgent.

"I didn't."

"Rylan, you asked to claim her. She's only known us two days. An hour ago she seemed certain you were going to hit her."

Rylan's wolf growled at that. "I never would."

"I know that. You know that. But she doesn't, not yet."

Sighing, Rylan admitted, "You're probably right. I got impatient." He rubbed his hand over his jaw. "The way she challenged me in front of the Alphas."

"She didn't know."

"They did."

"I want for us to be their Betas, too, Rylan. But we can't rush that either."

Rylan knew Chevy was right, but he lacked his brother's patience. They were so close to everything they'd wanted. Their mate in their life, *forever*, a place in the pack that they could be proud of. It was so close Rylan could almost taste it.

He sighed. "I'll be patient."

"Good. Then we should…" Chevy trailed off, looking toward the stairs. Rylan heard the footsteps, too, and a moment later Jarrod appeared at the head of the stairs.

"You're up late," Rylan said to the sheriff.

"Just checking the locks before I go to bed. I did a little research on your man Minogue, too."

"Did you find anything?"

"Nothing useful. If he's following Alyson, he's being a lot more careful than she was." Jarrod winced. "No offense."

"None taken," Chevy said. "Thanks for checking."

"We'll talk to Alyson and see if we can find anything more," Rylan said.

"I won't give up," Jarrod promised. "Good night."

They both wished Jarrod a good night. When the sheriff had continued down the hall, Rylan turned to his brother. "We good now?"

"Yeah. I just don't want to scare her now that we're so close."

"Believe me, I understand. Let's go back to our woman."

* * * *

"Are you sore, honey?" Tarkyn kissed her shoulder and rubbed her hip.

"No. I'm good."

"I want to make love with you, Alyson. Will you let me?"

Alyson gulped at the heated, hungry look her gave her. His eyes perused her body, halting at her breasts and then dropping to her pussy. Her clit throbbed, and her pussy clenched as if begging to be filled. Now that she knew the pleasure to be found in the act of lovemaking, her body craved more. But she knew she would only ever want these three men touching her.

Tarkyn reached out and thrummed his thumb over the elongated peak of her breast. An electrical zing shot down her body and centered in her pussy. As she clenched, more of her juice leaked out.

"Mmm, I can smell your cream, honey. Does that mean you want me, too?"

"Yes," Alyson sighed and turned from her side to her back.

Tarkyn slung a leg over her. Looming above her, he bracketed her body with his arms. He moved his legs, nudging hers apart to make room for himself, and then he blanketed her. His weight pressed her into the mattress, but he was careful not to crush her. He thrust his hips forward, his damp cock grinding into her mound. She closed her eyes and arched up, wanting to be filled with and surrounded by him.

He lowered his head and kissed her with such a hungry carnality that the embers of her desire stirred to flash fire in mere seconds. When she wrapped her arms around his shoulders to pull him close, he pushed one arm beneath her shoulders and the mattress and another around her hips and then rolled.

Alyson ended up on top of him, while he was on his back. Heat radiated from his body and seeped into hers while their lips remained locked together. His hand and fingers worked their way into her hair and cupped the back of her neck and head. Whether to prevent her from pulling away or for support, she had no idea, but at that moment she felt controlled and feminine. He was much larger than her and his size and strength made her feel delicate and sexy. His hand was so big it cradled the whole back of her head, and he was still able to caress the top of her spine with his long fingers.

She pulled back and gulped in air, trying to fill her oxygen-depleted lungs. When she looked into his eyes, the longing she saw in his depths caused her breath to hitch in her throat, and emotion swamped her. Tears pricked the backs of her eyes, but she lowered her eyelids to shield them from him. She belonged for the first time in her life and didn't know how to handle it. Blinking rapidly to dispel the tears, she looked up again when she had herself back under control. He helped her to sit up on his thighs and then pulled her forward until her crotch was aligned with his.

"You are so hot and wet," Tarkyn rasped. He touched a finger to her clit.

She tilted her head back and moaned as exquisite sensations washed over her. Alyson needed him inside her now. Using her legs, she pushed up and reached behind her to grasp his cock in her hand. He was soft and silky smooth. She salivated, wanting to taste him, to suck him into the depths of her mouth and lave his cock with her tongue, but she needed him inside her more. She yearned to make the same connection with Tarkyn and Chevy as she had with Rylan. The need was so strong she felt almost frantic with it.

Alyson rubbed the tip of his penis through her wet folds, coating the corona of his cock, and then she aligned him with her pussy hole. Slowly she lowered herself down onto him, panting for breath as the wide head of his rod spread her flesh open. He was so big she had to lift and lower over him five times before he was fully seated within her. She was slightly tender from making love for the first time, but the need to have him climax inside her negated anything else.

Tarkyn gripped her hip in one hand and held her still, allowing her to adjust to his intrusion, while the other continued to play with her pussy. He circled his finger around her small, sensitive bundle of nerves. When her pussy rippled and her clit was throbbing continuously, she couldn't hold back anymore. She rose up over him and tilted her hips slightly forward as she sank back down. With each flex of her legs she rode him harder and faster, undulating so that his cock stroked all the right places inside and out. Alyson twisted her hips slightly at the end of each downward plunge, drawing the shaft of his cock over her clit and enhancing her pleasure.

And then she froze. Another set of hands caressed from her shoulders down her back and over the cheeks of her ass. She looked over her shoulder to see Chevy staring at her ass intently. He looked up and met her gaze when she stopped moving.

"You are so damn sexy, darlin'. You have a gorgeous ass. Will you let me fuck it, Alyson?"

"W—What?"

"Chevy wants to make love with you, too, honey. Will you let us fuck you at the same time?" Tarkyn pushed his hips up at her and groaned when her internal muscles flexed around him.

The thought of having two men inside her at the same time made another surge of heat sweep through her. Her pussy rippled and dripped more cream.

"Oh, I think our mate likes that idea. Don't you, honey?"

"I—I…" The fantasy playing out in her mind stripped her of speech, but her body answered for her. Without conscious permission, her hips rolled forward, taking Tarkyn deeper.

Tarkyn reached out and gripped her shoulders. He pulled her down until her chest was flush with his. Her breasts pillowed up on his pectoral muscles as Chevy clasped the cheeks of her ass and kneaded them before spreading her wide. The slight stinging pain was a turn-on rather than a turn-off.

"Just relax, darlin'. I'll take good care of you. I promise." Chevy's voice sounded much deeper than normal.

The bed dipped near her knee, and Alyson turned her head toward the movement. Rylan was next to her, and as he began stroking her arm, he leaned down and kissed her forehead. A pop sounded, and Alyson tensed when cold liquid dribbled onto her ass. She drew in a gasp and shivered, but when she tried to move, firm, strong hands prevented her.

"Look at me, honey," Tarkyn demanded.

When she looked up, he gripped her hair and gave a slight tug toward him. She leaned forward, and then his mouth was on hers. He devoured her lips, sucking on her tongue, nipping her lower lip, and sweeping his tongue into every corner of her mouth. She mewled and slumped into him further as passion clawed at her.

Chevy massaged the lube into her anus, and then he pushed the tip of a finger inside. It was a foreign sensation, one she'd never thought to feel, but with these three men touching her and loving her, she craved more of everything they did to her. Dark excitement washed over her, causing more cream to leak from her vagina.

She moaned as Chevy pushed all the way into her back entrance and then wiggled his finger around, stretching her and adding to the pleasure of having a cock in her pussy. A whine escaped her lips when he pulled his finger from her anus, but that quickly turned to a squeak of appreciation when he came back with two.

For such a big man he was gentle. He took his time pushing through her tight sphincter muscles, stopping when she clenched and stretching her when she relaxed. All the time he prepared her, Tarkyn kissed her and held her still while Rylan caressed her back, shoulders, and arms. More lubrication was drizzled onto her back hole, and then the fullness escalated. There was a slight pinch and burn as he entered her with three fingers and stretched her out.

"You are such a good girl, darlin'," Chevy panted. "Now that you've taken three fingers, you're ready for my cock."

Alyson heard a squishy, moist sound and realized that Chevy was slathering his cock with lube. A small hand towel flew by her head on its way to the floor. She thought he must have used that to wipe his hand clean.

"I want you to stay very still, Aly. Don't move, because I don't want to hurt you. If it gets to be too much, you tell me right away. Okay?"

Alyson was apprehensive but so hungry to be filled she couldn't get her voice to work, so she nodded instead.

Chevy ran his cock over her asshole a few times while he gripped her shoulder with his hand. Then he began to push against her tight flesh. Even though she tried to relax, her natural instincts were to resist, and her ass clenched.

"Help her out, Tarkyn."

Alyson had no idea what Chevy meant until Tarkyn slipped a hand between their bodies and wiggled his finger around until he found her clit. He brushed it from side to side, massaging the engorged bundle of nerves at the top of her slit, and to her surprise her ass muscles loosened.

She mewled and groaned as the head of Chevy's cock pushed through the tight ring of muscle with a pop. His heavy breathing sounded loud in the quiet room. A drop of moisture plopped down onto her shoulder blade, and she realized that Chevy was sweating as he kept a tight rein on himself.

As his cock opened her virgin ass, the burn increased until she didn't think she would be able to stand it, but he went slow for her and stopped regularly, allowing her body to get used to him inside her. He withdrew a little and then pushed back in, gaining depth each time he moved forward, until he was all the way inside her, his pelvis against her butt cheeks.

"She's so fucking tight. I'm not gonna last long," Chevy groaned.

"Are you okay, baby?" Rylan pushed her hair away from her face.

"No! Move! Please," she sobbed. God, even *her* voice sounded deeper and more guttural than normal.

"You should have told me to stop if I was hurting you, Aly." Chevy sounded disappointed and began to ease from her ass.

"Stop," Alyson moaned. "I didn't mean you were hurting me, but I will hurt you if you both don't fuck me *now*!"

Tarkyn pushed up against her shoulders until she was sitting impaled on his cock and Chevy's front was against her back. She had a rapacious hunger and needed them to appease it. Alyson reached out almost blindly and gripped Rylan's cock in her hand. He was hard again, and she wanted to taste him. Using his dick as a handle, she pulled him forward until he got up on his knees with his erection close to her face. She opened her mouth wide and took him in.

"Fuck! Yeah, baby, suck on me. God, your mouth feels like heaven."

Alyson licked around the head of his cock and dipped her tongue into the eye of his dick. He tasted so good, like a combination of salt and musk. She wanted more. Chevy slowly withdrew his cock from her ass, and as he pushed back in, Tarkyn pulled from her pussy. She was so full, and it felt so right to have three men filling her holes, she went wild. Hollowing her cheeks, she sucked Rylan deep into her mouth until his corona touched the back of her throat. Though she loved him in her mouth, she gagged slightly and had to ease up. As she withdrew she gently scraped her teeth along the length of his shaft.

Chevy surged back into her ass as Tarkyn pulled out, and sparks of electricity zinged from her pussy to her ass up to her breasts and back down again. With each surge and retreat the two men filling her anus and cunt sped up incrementally, and she kept pace by bobbing up and down over Rylan's cock, laving the underside with her tongue. Their flesh slapped against hers and echoed through the room as if to the beat of an unseen drum. All of a sudden their rhythm began to falter and their thrusts became almost desperately uncoordinated.

From one heartbeat to the next, Alyson went from enjoying the pleasure being bestowed on her to standing on the precipice of another orgasm.

"Baby, let go. I'm gonna come."

She was only vaguely aware of what Rylan said since she was on the cusp of climax, too, but his words finally penetrated her endorphins-soaked brain. Reaching out, she cupped and squeezed his balls, and he shouted as his cock expanded and jerked in her mouth, spewing load after load of cum down her throat. She swallowed reflexively. She sucked him clean as he pulled from her mouth, and then he flopped down on the bed beside her, panting heavily.

"She's close," Tarkyn hissed through gritted teeth. "I can feel her rippling around me."

"Send her over," Chevy growled and then licked her shoulder.

Tarkyn placed the tips of two fingers on either side of her clit and then gently squeezed.

Alyson yelled as a tsunamic wave of rapture whirled through her body. Her pelvis muscles clamped down hard, gripping the cocks sliding in and out of her pussy and ass. Her whole body shook and shuddered. Cream gushed from her vagina and light seemed to flash all around her, and then she was fading with the last shake and shudder of her body. All her muscles went lax, and she knew no more.

Chapter Ten

Chevy caught Alyson around the waist so she wouldn't land on her face as she slumped forward.

"Alyson? Are you okay, darlin'?"

Tarkyn gently gripped her face between his hands and tilted her head so he could see her eyes. Chevy looked over her shoulder and leaned forward slightly so he could see her, too. Although she was still breathing more rapidly than normal, she appeared to be asleep.

"She passed out," Rylan said and sat up on the edge of the bed.

"So it would seem." Tarkyn eased her down, adjusting her head to rest on his shoulder.

"I'll go and fill the tub." Rylan walked toward the bathroom.

Chevy withdrew from her body with a groan, thankful the shaking in his legs had diminished enough to hold his weight. He followed Rylan into the bathroom to make sure everything was ready to wash their mate.

"She's special, isn't she?" Chevy looked at Rylan.

"Yeah," Rylan breathed, "more than she realizes."

"I feel like I'm already connected to her. I hope she lets us mate with her soon. This"—Chevy waved his hand toward the bedroom, where Tarkyn was currently holding their woman in his arms—"can only get better."

"God, I had a hard time not letting my wolf's instinct take over and claim her."

"Me, too." Rylan checked the bath water temperature. "But it will be much more intense and she will be more open with us by letting her make that decision when she's ready."

Chevy stared at Alyson sleeping in his brother's arms and thought of how fulfilled he and his brothers would feel if she accepted their mating claim. She'd already wormed her way into his heart, and it would kill him if she rejected him and his brothers.

After watching other members of their pack find and mate with their women, he'd been jealous, almost green with envy when he watched how the men took care of their women. If she let them claim her, he'd never have to feel like that again. Chevy prayed that Alyson would open up with them more. He felt that she was still holding part of herself back and that once she let herself just be with them, claiming her would seem less intimidating to her. He wanted her to let go and trust them, but Chevy knew trust had to be earned.

"Tub's ready." Rylan's voice drew him from his introspection.

Chevy walked back into the bedroom and picked Alyson up into his arms. It was such a comfort, so right to be able to hold her against him. If she'd allow it, he would spend hours cuddling her, but Alyson seemed to be one of those people who needed to be on the move all the time. She never sat totally still. Their little mate was always shifting, fidgeting with her fingers or her hair, or clasping her hands together. Now they had made love with her and showed her that she was safe, maybe she would begin to calm down.

After stepping into the bath, Chevy sat down with Alyson on his lap. She sighed and then moved her body, slowly awakening. Tarkyn and Rylan climbed into the tub and sat down on either side of him and their woman.

"Hey, baby. Welcome back." Rylan smoothed her hair away from her face.

"Hmm."

"How do you feel, honey?" Tarkyn ran a hand up and down her arm.

"Good."

"Are you sore, darlin'?" Chevy turned her until she sat with her back to his front.

"Yeah, just a bit." Alyson leaned her head back against his shoulder.

"Just relax and let us wash you, Aly." Rylan picked up a cloth and poured some bath gel onto it before handing it over to Tarkyn.

Chevy relished having her in his arms while his brothers bathed her. When they were done, he handed her off to Rylan after he'd dried off.

Five minutes later, they were all dried and back in the bedroom. Alyson's eyelids drooped, and Chevy knew sleep would claim her quickly, but his mind was back on what Jarrod had said in the hallway. It worried Chevy that there had been no progress on Virgil Minogue. Jarrod and his brothers were good at their jobs, but Virgil was well connected. If he slipped past the sheriff and his men, the pack might never see him coming.

Before Alyson lay down, Chevy touched her arm. "Alyson, Rylan and I spoke to Jarrod. He and his brothers haven't given up yet, but they can't find out anything helpful about Virgil Minogue." With the mention of that name, Alyson lost her sleepy look. Chevy regretted putting her on alert, but if there was anything else to tell Jarrod, he didn't want it to wait until morning. "Is there anything you can think of that we should know?"

"I've already told you everything I know. I don't have any more information for you."

"Have you contacted your old employer since you moved away from Phoenix?" Rylan asked.

"No. I was too scared to. The people working for him are computer savvy, and I didn't want him to trace my calls or e-mails. I'm afraid he'll follow up on his threat to shut the shelter down if I have any contact with them."

"I'll talk to Jarrod. It might be best if we let him get in touch with your previous employer. Did you buy a new cell phone when you moved?"

"No. Why would you ask me that?"

Chevy looked at Rylan and then over to Tarkyn. They both looked worried. He reached out and took her hand into his. "Darlin', weren't you aware that cell phones have GPS in them?"

"Umm, shit. I had no idea. Oh. My. God. Does that mean that my cell phone has been giving me away the whole time? He has probably known where I was since I left Phoenix?"

"Baby, calm down," Rylan said. "We'll turn off your phone and get you a new one. He won't be able to follow you then."

Alyson shook her head, her expression frantic. "It's too late. Oh God, you could all be in danger. I have to leave." Alyson let go of his hand, rose to her feet, and began to pace while gnawing on her lower lip.

"Stop, Alyson." Rylan stood, walked toward her, and placed his hands on her shoulders. "You aren't going anywhere. You are our mate. It is our job to protect you, not the other way around. Do you think this asshole is going to be able to get to you with us around? We are part wolf, which means we have heightened senses, baby. Our sense of smell is far better than a human's. Our eyesight is sharper, and we are stronger and faster. There is no way he can get to you. Plus, the rest of the pack will make sure you are safe, too."

"You have other women here, and there are children. I couldn't live with myself if something happened to them. You have to let me go."

"No fucking way," Chevy snapped. Alyson looked at him with shock on her face. He had shocked himself, too. Normally he was the mediator of the family and kept his brothers calm. Now it seemed having a mate to protect made him more dominant.

* * * *

Alyson stared at Chevy, who looked just as surprised as she felt. She'd never heard him talk so vehemently before. Chevy recovered from his surprise first and met her gaze with a stony look that was a lot like the one Rylan was giving her. But she was unconvinced. She could curse her oversight, but that didn't change the situation. She knew leaving was the right thing to do. She remembered baby Stefan sitting on Michelle's knee at the dining room table. The recollection brought back another mother and child. Virgil had tried to kill Mary's baby, and Alyson couldn't risk that he'd show up at the pack house and try to harm Michelle or Stefan. *He can't be allowed to hurt them. I have to go.* But she could tell by the fiercely determined expressions on all three men's faces that wasn't about to happen.

"You. Are. Not. Leaving," Rylan spoke between clenched teeth, but his voice was firm. "You are our mate. We want you to be our wife. What sort of men would we be if we let you go? This Virgil may already know you're here. What then, Alyson? As soon as you left the estate you would be in danger."

"Honey." Tarkyn's voice drew her eyes. "We have state-of-the-art security. No one can get in or out without the code, and if by chance the gates failed, we have cameras around the house and grounds. There is no way in hell someone could get in here without one of us knowing about it. We can scent a human from quite a distance. We would smell them before they even got close."

Alyson sighed and shrugged her shoulders, dislodging Rylan's hands from her body, and began to pace again. What they said made sense. But she was still worried. If Virgil was determined enough, he would find a way onto the grounds. Even if he managed to circumvent the security, there was no way he could avoid their noses.

She turned to look at them all and gripped her fingers and whispered, "I don't know if I'll stay."

"Yes, you will. There is no way I'm letting you leave," Rylan said in a steely voice.

"You are such an ass. There is no way you could keep me here if I didn't want to stay."

"Stop pushing me, Alyson. You may just find yourself over my knee."

"Are you threatening me?" She glared at Rylan.

"No, baby, that's a promise."

Alyson spun away and began to pace again.

"Sweetie, we're all tired," Tarkyn said. "Let's sleep on it and figure it out in the morning."

Almost in unison, Rylan growled and Chevy snapped, "No!"

"She needs to decide," Rylan said firmly.

Alyson looked him straight in the eye. *Could I bear to leave them?*

"What's it going to be?" Chevy asked.

All three of them looked tense as they awaited her answer. Their body language told her that they cared about her just as much as their words did. Nowhere else had she felt such a sense of belonging as she had with them.

So trust them when they say they'll protect you.

Alyson let out a sigh. It wasn't going to be easy to learn to lean on them, but she'd try. "I'll stay. For now."

Chevy and Tarkyn both smiled, but Rylan's expression stayed serious. Alyson found herself looking away from him as she got into bed.

If Virgil comes for me, I won't let him hurt anyone here. Even if it means leaving.

* * * *

Alyson came out of the bedroom and stopped. The three Friess brothers sat on the couch in the living room, dressed and looking as sexy as ever. She had woken up alone in bed, wondering if last night could really have happened.

Rylan stood up, enfolded her into his arms, and gave her a smoldering kiss.

That answers my question.

"Sleep well, baby?" he asked.

"Yeah. You guys should have woken me up. I didn't mean to sleep so late."

"It was kind of a long night," Tarkyn said with a grin.

"Breakfast is still being served downstairs." Chevy stood. "Let's go."

Alyson moved to follow him, but Rylan stopped her with a hand around her arm. "Baby, the whole pack will be at breakfast."

"Um, is that bad?"

"No. We want you to meet them. They're our family, and we'd like them to be your family, too."

That idea warmed Alyson's heart, but she read hesitance in Rylan's eyes. "So what's the problem?"

"You met Jonah and his brothers last night, and you saw what happened when you challenged one of us in front of them. Challenging the Alphas isn't a good idea either," Rylan said. "Jonah's word is Pack Law."

"I won't challenge anybody," Alyson promised.

"Then let's go. I'm hungry," Chevy said.

Tarkyn opened the suite door. Following him down the hall with the others behind her, Alyson asked, "Not that I'm going to do anything to get you in trouble, but what happens if you challenge the Alphas?"

"Our Alphas are pretty lenient, actually," Tarkyn said, "especially with newcomers. But because he is our most dominant and oldest Alpha, Jonah can use his voice to compel the pack to obey him. He doesn't use it often, but when he does, everyone has to submit to his will and follow whatever directive he has given."

"Huh, that must come in handy."

"Only when necessary. We can use our voices, too, if we want, but only on our mate, and only after we've claimed you. All the mated wolves have the power to compel their mate to do their will."

Alyson stopped dead in her tracks. "That means you could make me—"

Tarkyn turned and looked at her. "I haven't finished yet, Alyson. Hear me out before you get too riled up."

I'm an independent woman. They can't make me do anything with their voices if I don't—

Tarkyn swept her up in his arms, making her squeak with surprise. He smiled. "If you won't walk, I'll just have to carry you."

"I can walk. I'm not an invalid."

"We know you aren't, baby. But we want to take care of you. You are our mate," Rylan said from behind them as they walked down the hall.

Tarkyn continued his explanation as if there had been no interruption. "The only time a wolf uses his voice on his mate is if her life is in danger. At no other time will we use that power over you."

That was good to know, but all this talk about claiming made her realize how much she still didn't know about the Friess brothers and their pack. "Will I turn into a werewolf once you claim me?"

"No, darlin'," Chevy said. "You have to be born with the Lycan gene to be able to shift, or you have to be turned, and there is no way in hell we would do that to you."

"Why?"

"It is a horrific experience for a human to be changed. A wolf has to bite deeply enough to get the werewolf DNA into the human's body. It's the only way for the gene to be activated. Keira, who you'll meet downstairs, and Rochelle both had to be changed. Those two women are damn lucky to be alive."

Alyson shuddered, snuggling into Tarkyn. She rested her cheek against his hard chest and breathed in his wonderfully unique, masculine scent. "It's not something you have to worry about," Tarkyn said as he descended the stairs.

"Right, I just have to worry about meeting a bunch of werewolves and not challenging any of them," she grumbled.

At the bottom, he finally set her down. Thinking about meeting the pack made her realize another question. When Tarkyn tugged on her hand, she stayed put. "What is it, sweetie?"

She looked between the three of them, her gaze coming to rest on Rylan. "Why aren't you guys the Alphas?"

Chevy was the one who answered. "Jonah and his brothers earned the title. We hope to someday be their Betas and help them run the pack."

"Someday," Rylan repeated. There was a sour note in his voice, but before Alyson could ask, he took her hand and tugged her toward the dining room. "Let's eat."

She could hear voices and the sounds of cutlery on plates from the dining room, and it sounded like a lot of people were in there. Nerves made her stomach flutter. Alyson wanted to make a good first impression on the Friess brothers' pack, the people who might someday be her family.

Girl, don't mess this up.

Taking a deep breath, she followed her men into the dining room.

Chapter Eleven

Alyson sat down in her chair at the dining room table with a sigh. After being introduced to the whole pack, she was ready to eat. She was amazed by the number of people filling the room, and her mind was spinning from learning so many new names. She hoped she wouldn't offend anyone by calling them the wrong name.

As she and the Friess brothers had made the rounds, she had noticed that there were far more men than women in the dining room. Initially, that unnerved her, but she'd already seen many examples of how the men treated their women. Watching the Alphas playing with Stefan at the head of the table warmed her heart and body. Never had she seen such love and devotion. Not only that, but all of their mates had backbone. Even if the women were few, they clearly weren't afraid of the huge specimens of masculinity that surrounded them.

Jarrod and his brothers were sitting across the table from her and her men with Rochelle. Alyson noticed that Rochelle was the only person not eating meat for breakfast besides herself.

"I'm glad to see I'm not the only one averse to eating meat." Rochelle smiled at her.

"Oh, I don't mind eating it, just not for breakfast."

"Huh, and here I thought I finally had someone on my side for a change." Rochelle glared at Jarrod. "These big lugs can't understand all my little idiosyncrasies."

"Hey." Jarrod tapped Rochelle on the nose. "You know damn well that's not true. We've done everything we can to see you have the food you need and want."

"I know." Rochelle gave a giggle. "I was just teasing you."

Alyson gave Rochelle another smile and watched as the woman got to her feet. She was still talking to her mate as she walked and didn't seem to see Angela and Cindy carrying large platters of food toward the table. Rochelle was headed right for them.

"Look out!" Alyson sprang from her seat ready to help, but she wasn't needed. Jarrod moved so fast he was a blur. He swept Rochelle up into his arms and stepped back.

"God, baby. What am I going to do with you? You could have been hurt. Again!"

"I know." Rochelle sighed. "Lucky for me I have three big, brawny men to keep me safe."

Jarrod put his mate down carefully. "Let me run upstairs and get your purse, and then we can go to work." He kissed her forehead. "I'll be right back."

Rochelle turned back to Alyson with a slightly sheepish smile. "I don't know what I'd do without them."

Alyson tried to smile back, but she was fighting a strange new sense of envy. What would it be like to have that kind of bond with a man—or three? "You work with him?"

"I'm the dispatcher for the sheriff's department." Rochelle suddenly grew solemn, and she leaned closer and placed a reassuring hand over Alyson's. "Don't worry, Alyson. We'll find him."

Last night had been so amazing that all thought of Virgil Minogue had been swept from her mind when she woke this morning. The danger she was in, the danger she'd put *all* of them in, came crashing back down on her. "Thanks," she managed to squeak.

Jarrod returned then with Rochelle's purse, and they headed out of the dining room.

Alyson watched her go. Virgil was upsetting her life in more ways than one. Last night, Jerry had made it clear that Alyson was out of a job until she was safe. Her blood boiled thinking about the job she was no longer "allowed" to do, but the Friess brothers seemed determined to hold her to it, and she had to agree that driving a truck all over New Mexico might put her in harm's way. Yet she hated being idle.

She shifted in her seat as her men worked their way through the pile of food on their plates. Alyson couldn't believe how much food they put away, but it seemed a werewolf's metabolism was much faster than a human's, so they needed more fuel to sustain their bodies. She gripped her hands tightly around her mug of coffee and sighed.

"What's wrong, baby?" Rylan turned to her and scrutinized her face.

"What am I going to do now that you and Jerry won't let me work? I can't just sit around and do nothing."

"I've been thinking about that." Tarkyn placed his silverware on his plate and gently rubbed her back. "We have to be at the club in a couple of hours. If you'd like, you can come and help out behind the bar."

"Well, I guess I could do that. It would be better than sitting around here, idle."

"Good." Rylan pushed his empty plate away. "But you have to stay inside. We don't want you going anywhere without one of us with you."

"Sure." Alyson sighed again. She wasn't used to having her freedom curtailed, but until they knew where Virgil was and what he was up to, it was better to be safe than sorry.

* * * *

Alyson grabbed an empty tub and walked about clearing dirty glasses, plates, and pitchers from tables. The lunch rush hour was over, thank goodness, and her feet were aching from moving so quickly. She'd been helping Rylan and Tarkyn behind the bar while Chevy dealt with orders and invoices. Moving the full tub of dirty dishes aside, she sprayed the tables with disinfectant and cleaned them off. She was about to take the dishes into the kitchen when she caught a glimpse of a man walking past the window in the mirror on the far wall. Turning quickly, she tried to see if it was who she thought, but it was too late. The man had already passed the window.

Dumping the tub onto another table, she rushed over to the window and peered out, but she didn't see anyone who even resembled Virgil. *It probably wasn't him to begin with.* He was a pretty nondescript guy, and she'd only glimpsed him for a second. Telling herself not to be so paranoid, she took the dirty dishes into the kitchen and began to load the dishwasher.

Chevy was sitting at a table off to the side of the room near the entrance to the hall, eating and going over some more papers. He glanced over to her, frowned, and opened his mouth to speak. Then he snapped it closed again when he noticed the kitchen staff looking at her curiously through the kitchen door. *What's up with them?*

"Aly, when you've finished with the dishes I'd like to see you in my office," Chevy called out as he picked up his papers and moved down the hallway. He waited for her answer.

"Okay." Alyson wondered for a moment what Chevy wanted but then figured he was probably going to question her about rushing over to peer out the window. There was no way she was creating an opening for gossip about her. She was having enough trouble fitting in with the kitchen staff and trying to win over Cherry, who had seemed to take an instant dislike to her. Ever since Cherry had arrived that morning, she had been giving Alyson venomous looks. It didn't take a genius to figure out the waitress had had her sights set on her mates. Once finished, she headed out to see Chevy. Just as she turned the corner into the hallway, Cherry's voice carried to her hearing.

"God, I hope that bitch gets the sack."

"Cherry, sheathe your claws, girl," Joanne, the cook, said. "You don't stand a chance. Haven't you noticed the way our three bosses watch every move she makes?"

"She can't have them all." Cherry's voice faded away.

That's what you think, bitch. Alyson sniggered to herself. They were her mates and hadn't looked at Cherry twice even when she'd tried to flirt with her men, but she wasn't about to rub her relationship in the other woman's face. On the other hand, Alyson wasn't going to hold back if Cherry wanted to pick a fight with her. She'd heard more snide remarks from the redhead in the last couple of hours than she'd heard in the past year. Cherry wore her jealousy on her sleeve, but she was too clueless to be a real threat. Earlier today Alyson had overheard Rylan chewing her out for leaving food on one of the counters overnight and spoiling it. Cherry had tried to flirt her way out of the mistake, but Rylan had been having none of it.

Alyson entered the office to see Chevy waiting for her. She stood in front of his desk.

"What's the problem?"

Chevy leaned back in his chair and crossed his arms over his wide chest. His biceps bulged beneath the seams on his T-shirt sleeves. "I was hoping you could tell me that."

"What do you mean?"

The relaxed pose gone, Chevy leaned forward and studied her intently. "Your face was as pale as a ghost when you walked toward the kitchen with the dirty dishes and your hands were shaking. I could feel and smell the fear emanating from you."

Shit! "Why do you have to be able to see things like that? I won't ever have any privacy if you can all smell my emotions."

"Get used to it, baby. Now answer the question," he demanded.

"You are such an ass."

"That may be, baby, but I'm your ass now. So deal. I'm still waiting." Chevy pushed his chair back and rose to his feet. The way his muscles rippled as he moved made her blood sing with desire. She would never get tired of being near them.

"I thought I saw Virgil pass by the window." Alyson sighed with resignation and nervously rubbed her palms down the sides of her jeans-clad thighs. "I had my back to the window but I thought I caught a glimpse of him in the mirror on the back wall. But when I turned, he was gone. I even went and looked out, but he was nowhere to be seen. I guess after talking about him last night with your cousins, it got me a bit paranoid and jumpy."

"Why didn't you say something?" Chevy asked in a cool voice.

Alyson flung her hands up and then wrapped her arms around her waist. "Because I wasn't even sure it was him."

Rylan hurried into the office with Tarkyn close behind. He walked right up to her until the toes of his boots were touching the tips of her shoes, making her tilt her head back so she could see his face. She wished she hadn't when she saw how angry he looked. *Will I ever get used to them being able to hear me even when they're not in the same room?*

"The next time you think you see Virgil, you let one of us know. You are in danger, for fuck's sake, Alyson. When are you going to let that independence go and let us help you?"

"I need more time. God, I've only known you a few days and I already want you—" She stopped herself. They didn't need to know she was considering letting them claim her and make her theirs. Changing tack, she went on, "I can't just let habits of a lifetime go. I'm not used to relying on anyone else but myself. It probably wasn't even Virgil Minogue that I saw walking past. It was probably just a man with similar height and hair color."

"What does he look like?" Chevy asked. "What was he wearing?"

"Um, dress slacks, I think." She racked her memory. "Navy-blue shirt. Oh, he had a black jacket slung over his shoulder. He looks like any other executive type."

"What's his build like?" Chevy asked.

"He's about six feet, maybe a hundred and eighty pounds. Black hair with gray at the temples, about collar length." She sighed. "Of course, that was a year ago, when I saw him last. He could look totally different by now. And that probably wasn't him."

"Whether or not it was him, Alyson, you should have said something," Rylan said in a hard voice. "You will come to one of us the next time. Do I make myself clear?"

"Crystal!" Alyson snapped and glared at him. When he just continued to hold her gaze, she knew she wasn't going to be the winner of this showdown. She lowered her head and moved around him then out the office door and rounded the corner into the hall. Her body bumped into another and she gripped the other woman's arms to stop her from falling.

"Sorry, Cherry, I didn't mean to smack into you. Are you okay?"

"Fine," Cherry ground out from between clenched teeth.

"Were you looking for me?"

"No. Why would I want to find you?" Cherry looked her up and down as if Alyson was something she had stepped in. "I need to speak to the managers."

Alyson kept her face blank and made her way back to the bar, but inside she cursed Cherry with every step. She slid in behind the bar on the opposite end from Carter, one of the younger pack members who worked there through the week, and began to fill orders. She worked her way down and gave Carter a smile when they met in the middle. Lucky for her mates she'd spent some time working in a restaurant and knew what she was doing. It was Friday, and things were really beginning to hop as it got closer to dinnertime.

Every once in a while Alyson looked toward the hallway and kept an eye out for her three men. They hadn't shown their faces at the bar since that confrontation earlier in the afternoon, and she wondered what they were doing. *Are they still talking about me? Have they had some news about Virgil? God, why do I care what they are doing so much?* Alyson couldn't believe how quickly she had grown to depend on them. It felt like there was an empty hole in her heart, and she knew only those three could fill it. And they hadn't even claimed her yet. Would that make her feel more complete? Would it be harder to stay away from them?

The desire to stay with them and be a part of their lives grew the more she got to know them. Maybe tonight they could talk about it some more, she thought. She could apologize for not telling them about seeing Virgil and ask all her questions about life in the pack.

After helping Carter with the drink orders, Alyson did another sweep of the tables, collecting more dirty dishes, and took them into the kitchen. She spied Cherry at the back door. She was half in and half out of the entrance, and it looked like she was talking to someone while she smoked a cigarette. The stench wafted into the kitchen, making Alyson crinkle her nose with distaste. As she approached to ask Cherry to close the door, Cherry looked over her shoulder. Her face seemed to drain of color and then went bright red.

What's with her? Maybe she feels bad to be caught smoking?

Cherry quickly stepped outside and closed the door behind her. Alyson gave a mental shrug and got back to her chores.

* * * *

He had bided his time, and his patience had paid off.

You can't get rid of me by turning off your cell phone. The phone's GPS and Virgil's connections had gotten him as far as Aztec, but his target had disappeared before he could close in. It was just his luck. Ten months of searching fruitlessly for Mary had given him a taste for failure, but he wouldn't fail any longer. The bitch from the shelter might have hidden Mary too well for him to find her again, but Virgil now knew exactly where to find Alyson Redding.

When he'd lost the GPS signal, he'd switched to plan B. This morning he'd questioned one of the delivery drivers from the warehouse in Bloomfield, the one where his contacts told him she'd last been hired to work. He'd missed her only by a day, but the driver said she wouldn't be around anymore. When he'd offered the other driver cash, the young man had told him he'd overheard his boss on the phone and she was now working and living in Aztec.

Now, at last, he'd gotten lucky. When he had seen her through that window he'd thought for a moment he had conjured her from his imagination.

Sneering with glee and rubbing his hands together, he walked around to the rear of the building, making plans. She had to pay for taking his family away. Now he had no one, not even his job. If it hadn't been for that bitch Alyson, he would still have everything. She had to pay for what she'd done to him.

He was so much better than anyone else. Who did the slut think she was, helping his wife and daughter to leave him? He didn't really care about his job or colleagues. It was the principle of the situation he found himself in. He was lucky he had more than enough money to live off the interest for the rest of his life if he wanted to, thanks to the money his parents had bequeathed him at their deaths and his acumen with investments. What he lacked was a way to close in on his prey. Alyson Redding was safely inside the Aztec Club, which seemed to be full of huge, fierce-looking men. Brute force wouldn't get her out of there. Virgil needed another way.

The rear door to the club opened just as he entered the alley, and a redhead stood on the top step and lit a smoke. *Yes, this is perfect. It was meant to be.* He approached the dour-looking woman and pasted a smile onto his face.

"Hi there, I was wondering if you knew Alyson Redding?"

She looked him up and down, eying his designer watch and clothes. A smile spread over her face, replacing the hard look she had first given him. "Why do you want *her*?"

"She's my cousin," he lied. "I have some bad news regarding a family member and didn't want to have to tell her over the phone."

"Oh, too bad," the woman said insincerely. "She doesn't get a break for another two hours. If you can wait, I'll bring her out after the dinner hour."

"Thank you. I'd appreciate it. Have you got a cell phone?"

"Yeah. What of it?"

"If you would allow me to give you my cell number, you can call or text me just before you bring her out. I want to go to the motel and reserve a room."

"Sure."

"I don't want her upset without me by her side to offer comfort."

Cherry turned her head, exhaling smoke. Something seemed to catch her attention out of the corner of her eye. She looked back over her shoulder, her eyes widened, and she hastily shut the door into the club.

"What was that?" Virgil asked. "Did someone hear us?"

"It was nothing." Cherry had a calculating look on her face. "Since I'm being so helpful, don't I deserve a reward?"

He gazed at her silently for a moment. He had a suspicion that Alyson had been on the other side of the door just now and that Cherry had deliberately blocked him from seeing her. The bitch wasn't as dumb as she looked, he reflected.

The fact remained that she was his best way to get to Alyson so far. Reaching into his jacket, he pulled out his checkbook. When he'd written the check and handed it to Cherry, he asked, "Is that satisfactory?"

Her eyes widened. "Uh...yeah...Virgil Minogue, that's your name?"

"Keep that to yourself," he said, "and maybe there's another check in it for you."

Cherry folded the check and stuffed it in her bra. She gave him a simpering smile. "Okay."

She's mine now.

He bid her good-bye and watched as she went back inside. He was going to have to prepare quickly since he hadn't expected to find her so fast.

Chapter Twelve

Alyson took a seat at the bar and sipped her mineral water. Her feet were aching from spending the last two hours rushing about. She was glad the kitchen was now closed and only the bar was open. She was used to being on her feet, but it had been quite a few years since she had worked in a bar or hotel, and she wasn't used to the pace. Delivering was so much easier. Although there was less heavy lifting in this job.

Rylan and Tarkyn were now working behind the bar with Carter and she was glad to be on her break. The people waiting for drink orders to be filled were three deep. Chevy walked down the hallway and slipped in behind the gleaming mahogany bar to help his brothers and employee. He leaned over and gave her a kiss on the forehead while he pulled beer from the tap.

"Are you okay, darlin'?"

"Yes," Alyson replied in a raised voice so he could hear her over the din and chatter from the crowd. "I'm just a bit weary."

"Why don't you go and sit at the small table in the kitchen, where it'll be less noisy?" Chevy suggested and placed the glasses in front of the patrons and took their money. "I can see you have a headache."

"How do you do that?"

"Your eyelids are narrowed and you have a frown. I can see the pain in your eyes."

Alyson sighed but gave a nod and slid off her barstool. "You know where to find me if you want more help."

Just as she started down the hallway Cherry was walking toward her.

"Alyson, I need your help."

Sighing with frustration and pain, Alyson hid a cringe as Cherry's high-pitched voice grated on her nerves.

"What do you need?"

"Can you take the garbage out back to the Dumpster, please? I still have to wipe down the stove, grill, and counters."

Alyson followed Cherry into the kitchen and saw the three garbage bags near the door to the alley. She opened the door and picked up two bags. Just as she dumped them she caught movement in her peripheral vision and half turned. She cried out when a fist connected with her jaw. Pain radiated out from her jaw and up into her head. She staggered as her vision began to blur. Virgil Minogue's image wavered before her eyes and her muscles turned to lead. With a cry of fear and helplessness, she fell to the ground and stared up at her nemesis before she sank down into a pain-induced sleep.

* * * *

Rylan glanced toward the kitchen for the umpteenth time that night. It had been an hour since Alyson had left the bar, and he was becoming concerned that she hadn't come back. He didn't care if she didn't work for the rest of the night, but he and his wolf needed her close. His animal was becoming antsy. Cherry and the kitchen staff had left over thirty minutes ago, and still there was no sign of his mate.

"Chevy, what was Alyson doing?"

"She had a headache and went to the kitchen to get away from the noise in here."

"Was she going to come back out here to help clean up?"

Chevy shrugged. *"I don't know, but she did tell me to call if we wanted or needed her help."*

"Alyson, are you all right, baby?" Rylan called to his mate as he walked down the hall.

Nothing.

"Tarkyn, have you seen Aly?" Rylan asked his brother after a quick glance in the kitchen. He turned back toward the bar and began to fill another drink order.

"Not since she was sitting on that stool."

"Fuck!" Rylan handed the glass he had been filling with beer to Chevy and moved quickly back toward the kitchen. He stopped in the doorway again and used his wolf senses to sniff her out, but she wasn't there and her scent was weak, as if she hadn't been there for some time. Turning on his heel, he walked toward the office. Empty. He walked further along the hall to the staff restrooms, and after tapping on each door and getting no answer, he opened first the ladies' bathroom and then the men's. They were both unoccupied.

"She's not here." Rylan tried to contain his panic.

"What do you mean she's not here? She has to be." Tarkyn met him in the kitchen.

"Chevy, get some of the young weres *to help Carter behind the bar. Our mate is missing."*

"Shit."

Rylan used his wolf senses and inhaled deeply. Alyson's scent was most prevalent near the rear door. He opened it and stepped out and could smell that she had been near the Dumpster. Mixed in with her natural aroma was garbage and human male.

"I'm going to shift." Rylan began to remove his clothes and handed them to Tarkyn just as Chevy came outside. "I'm getting a trace of a male. My wolf will be able to scent it better."

Rylan called to his wolf and let his human side slide away. When the shift was complete, he sniffed the area. He inhaled, taking the man scent in deep so his animal would remember the odor. Whoever he was, Rylan could tell he was bad news to his mate.

"Alyson was here and a human male. My guess is that it was this Virgil Minogue or someone he hired."

"Fuck it!" Tarkyn roared. "We need to contact Jarrod and his brothers."

"I'm on it." Chevy drew his cell phone from his pocket and dialed. "Jarrod, we have a problem. Alyson is missing. We followed her trail to the back alley behind the club, but there's the smell of a human male, too. We think she's been abducted."

"Shit." Rylan heard Jarrod's voice loud and clear. "We'll be there in a minute."

Chevy disconnected the call. "Can you follow the trail and see where this asshole took her?"

Rylan took off, keeping his nose to the ground. He was careful to keep to the shadows as he skirted cars in the parking lot at the end of the alley, his brothers jogging to keep up with him. He stopped at an empty parking space and growled low in his throat with frustration.

"The trail ends here. Whoever he was, he had a car waiting."

Tires screeched nearby. Rylan's brothers stood in front of him to shield him from being seen, but the truck belonged to the Aztec sheriff's department. Rylan relaxed slightly as Jarrod bounded out of the truck.

"Virgil Minogue is clean, but I also called Jerry to see if he knew anything. He knows about as much as we do, but he wants me to call him back if we need him to help find Alyson. I have Malcolm and Braxton out combing the area. If they sight him, we'll know in moments." Jarrod pointed to the radio strapped to his shoulder.

"I feel so fucking helpless. We have no idea where this asshole would have taken her. God, I just want to hold her." Rylan headed back to the alley and changed back to human form. Tarkyn handed him his clothes, and he got dressed.

The fear at not having Alyson close and the pain in his heart at her being in danger was almost debilitating. He needed to wrap himself around her and never let go.

* * * *

Alyson's head was pounding, and so was her jaw. The skin on her lower face felt tight and swollen, and her mouth felt like the bottom of a bird's cage. Consciousness returned slowly, and she tried to remember why she felt so bad. Trying to get her eyelids to open took way more effort than it should have, but when she finally got them up, she couldn't see anything anyway. *Where the hell am I? What is going on?*

She tried to move her arms to push herself up into a sitting position, but when she tugged, they held fast. *Fuck! I'm tied up and lying on my back.* Moving her legs produced the same result. Her breath hitched in her throat with fear. Her heart raced and she began panting heavily as anxiety took over. She wanted to flee, but she couldn't move.

Then she remembered the dream she'd had of Virgil punching her in the jaw and standing over her while she lay on the ground looking up at him before she lost consciousness.

Oh my God. It wasn't a dream. You are in deep shit, girl, if that asshole has you.

Alyson squirmed and tugged the ropes around her wrists and ankles. They abraded her skin, but she ignored the pain and kept pulling. Her flesh tore and through the pain she felt the warmth of blood on her skin, but she wasn't going to give in. She had to escape or she would end up dead. But she would die before she gave that fucking asshole any information on Mary and her baby.

Where are my mates? Do they even know I'm missing? How long have I been gone? Will I ever see them again? Alyson thought of Rylan, Tarkyn, and Chevy, stifling the sob working its way up her chest to her throat. She had no idea where she was and couldn't get her hands out of the rope. She realized that she may never see them again and she hadn't even told them she loved them. Now she may never get the chance.

A squeak let her know the door was being opened, and then light filtered in from behind her closed eyelids, but she listened intently as whoever was there got closer to her. She tried not to flinch when a hand touched her face, but she must have moved infinitesimally because male laughter filled the room.

"I know you're awake, bitch, so you can stop the act."

A hand slapped her face, and she cried out as pain radiated from her cheek up to her eye and into her already-throbbing jaw and head.

Alyson opened her eyes and faced her enemy.

* * * *

Tarkyn was beside himself with worry for Alyson. He didn't know how much more waiting he could stand. He and his brothers were in the Aztec Club office, waiting to hear from Malcolm and Braxton for news on Virgil and their mate. Jarrod was sitting at the desk, typing rapidly on the keyboard. Tarkyn felt so useless and helpless and wanted to be out there searching for his woman. He hated that he and his brothers had to wait for information from Jarrod and his brothers, but until they knew where to head, there was nothing else they could do. It would be fruitless to go out searching for Alyson. If they headed in the wrong direction, precious time would be wasted when they had to backtrack. His chest hadn't stopped aching from the moment they realized Alyson was missing, and he rubbed it again as he stood up and began to pace.

Chevy watched him move from his seat on the sofa, and Rylan was on the phone to Jonah. Their Alpha was going to alert all the pack members to keep an eye out for Virgil and Alyson.

Just as Tarkyn was about to declare he couldn't take any more and was going to look for his woman, Jarrod's radio went off.

"Jarrod, his car's been found."

"Where?"

The voice coming from the radio was Malcolm's. "Jerry was out in the next town over and spotted Alyson in the front seat of his car. He followed them for a while, being careful to stay back so he wouldn't be seen. He called it in a minute ago. It's at an abandoned farmhouse half an hour west of the den."

"Shit. I know exactly where you mean. Call in reinforcements from the pack, but no one is to go in until I get there. Wait." Jarrod turned to Rylan. "Are you still on the phone with Jonah?

"Yes."

"Tell him we have the bastard and we want Blayk there in case we need his medical expertise."

Tarkyn's heart stuttered at the thought of Alyson being injured and in pain. He took a deep breath as his wolf pushed against him, urging him to start looking for their mate.

"Okay."

"Is Braxton with you?" Jarrod asked Malcolm over the police radio.

"Yeah, I'm here, big brother."

"Good. I want you both to get close to the house and see what's going on. If you need to go in before we arrive, then do it. Alyson's life is more important than having her mates on standby."

"Understood."

"Let's go." Tarkyn headed toward the door.

"Wait up." Jarrod caught up to him and placed a hand on his shoulder. "You three can ride with me. I don't want you getting in the way and putting yourself in the line of fire. The last thing I need is any of you getting hurt."

"Fuck, Jarrod, you know I would be careful. If we're hurt, we can't protect Alyson," Tarkyn snarled.

"Control your wolf, man. Take a few deep breaths and calm down. You aren't going to do any good if you don't get a handle on your emotions."

Tarkyn breathed deeply and pushed his animal down as he followed Jarrod and his brothers out to Jarrod's truck. As they sped through the night, he thought about how much he loved Alyson and how distraught he and his brothers would be if they lost her.

No! He pushed those negative thoughts aside. They weren't going to lose her. They had only just found her. He would give his life without a qualm if needed. She was the love of their lives, and nothing was going to come between them.

His thoughts brought his wolf back to the surface and his claws pushed from the ends of his fingers while he growled from deep in his chest. Rylan and Chevy's growls joined his. The trip, which should have taken at least thirty minutes, took fifteen. He was glad Jarrod knew how to control his vehicle at such high speeds.

He was out of the car before Jarrod had stopped completely and ripped his clothes from his body. The change was so fast his bones ached, but he embraced his animal. Two more wolves came up alongside him and Rylan and his brothers all ran toward the farmhouse in the distance.

"I told you three to wait," Jarrod sent through the common pack link, but they ignored him. *"Shit!"*

"What can you see, Malcolm?" Rylan asked.

"From what I can see, he has her tied up to an old bed in the back bedroom of the house. Brax and I had to move back so he wouldn't see us. He got too close to the broken window. He hit her, but we didn't want to go in yet. She's been talking to him and trying to get him to calm down, but he has a gun. If he sees us, he could fire a bullet into her heart or head and kill her."

"Cover us," Rylan ordered.

Tarkyn didn't bother to stop or slow down once the house was in sight. He ran around back and saw light emanating through a broken window. He peered through the dirty glass and barely kept his wolf under control. If he or his brothers jumped through the window, he was scared the fucker would pull the trigger and kill their mate.

"Where is my wife and baby, bitch?" Virgil snarled and pushed the barrel of the gun hard against Alyson's head.

Alyson whimpered and tears flowed from her eyes, and to Tarkyn's horror she spat in Virgil's face and yelled, "Fuck you!"

Virgil backhanded Alyson across the face, which caused her to cry out in pain, and it was a real struggle for him and his brothers not to jump through the window and try to save their mate. What they needed was a distraction. If they could somehow lure Virgil away from Aly, then they would be able to save her without her getting shot.

"Jarrod, we need a distraction. He has a gun to her head," Tarkyn said through the common pack link.

"Okay, I'm on it."

As the minutes ticked by Tarkyn and his animal were filled with rage, and the struggle for supremacy between his human and animal side was imperative. If his wolf took over, he could get his mate killed.

"Tell me where my wife is and I'll let you go." Virgil ran the gun barrel down the side of Aly's head and then pushed it hard beneath her chin.

Alyson sobbed, but then he heard her take a deep breath as if she was gathering herself back under control. When she spoke this time her voice was full of fury. "Do you think I'm stupid? I know damn well you aren't going to let me leave here alive. So why don't you just get it over with and pull the fucking trigger."

Tarkyn mentally growled. Once they got her out of there and she had recovered he was going to put Alyson over his knee and spank her ass for goading a crazy man into trying to kill her.

The sound of flesh slapping against flesh was sickening. Ire and fear raged a battle inside his chest, and he urged Jarrod on. *"Hurry the fuck up. She's trying to make him kill her."*

Just as Tarkyn finished yelling through the link, a car alarm sounded from the front of the cabin. Virgil stiffened and pulled the gun away from Alyson's face. He flicked the safety on and pushed the gun into the waistband of his pants. That was just what Tarkyn had been waiting for.

He leapt. Jagged glass cut into his belly, but he didn't feel any pain. Virgil spun toward the window and reached for the weapon, but Tarkyn was faster.

His front and back paws barely touched the floor before they left the wood again. Rylan and Chevy jumped through the window after him. He didn't hesitate to let his wolf have free reign. His animal bit down hard as his teeth closed around Virgil Minogue's arm. He heard the thud of the gun hitting the floor and knew that his mate was safe. With a snarl he released the fucker's arm and went for his throat. The flesh gave beneath his teeth and he shook his head back and forth violently. Blood filled his mouth, and his teeth sank even further into muscle, cartilage, and sinew. When he felt the life leave the human and the body go slack, he threw it aside without a care.

His mate needed him.

Chapter Thirteen

Chevy rushed over to Alyson as soon as his paws hit the floor. Her face was bruised, the skin around her wrists and ankles was shredded, and she was naked, but she was alive. He forced his wolf back and allowed his human side to take over. As soon as he changed, he undid the rope and pulled her into his arms.

"Aly, you're safe now, darlin'. We have you. God, I love you so much."

"Chevy?" she asked in a shaky voice.

"Yes, darlin', I'm here." Chevy pulled her tight against him, sharing the warmth from his body. Her skin was very cold and her whole body was shaking. She wrapped her arms around his waist and held on tight while she sobbed. He glanced up to see Tarkyn wiping the blood from his body, and then his brother covered Virgil's mangled body with an old blanket. Chevy would have held her on his lap if she'd let him, but she sat up when she heard Jarrod and his brothers' voices.

"I'm naked," Alyson whispered. "I don't want them to see me like this."

Chevy didn't want his cousins seeing his mate's body either. He searched the room, but the only useful thing he could see was the dirty quilt on the old bed, and he wasn't about to use that on his precious woman.

"Jarrod"—Chevy raised his voice slightly, knowing Jarrod would hear him even though his cousin was still outside—"do you have a spare set of clothes? Alyson needs them."

"I'll get them." Tarkyn, who had moved away from Virgil and had been stroking Alyson's hair, walked toward the door. "Don't come in. Aly doesn't want you guys seeing her naked. Did you bring our clothes, too?"

Tarkyn's arms were full of clothes when he turned back around. He handed over some sweatpants and a shirt to Chevy, and he helped Alyson dress, rolling up the sleeves of the shirt and the legs of the pants so they didn't irritate her torn skin.

"Okay, she's decent. Send Blayk in," Rylan ordered as he dressed.

Chevy handed her over to Rylan so he could dress. He watched as Blayk cleaned and bandaged her wounds. When he was done, Tarkyn picked her up and began to walk out of the house.

"Wait!" Alyson cried. "Tarkyn, put me down."

"Why?"

"Because you have a cut on your stomach. You need to let Blayk look at that."

"Pfft. It's just a scratch, honey. It'll be healed by the time we get back to Jarrod's truck."

"God, I still have so much to learn about you guys." Alyson looked up to Tarkyn then over to him and finally to Rylan.

"Thank you all for saving me. If it hadn't been for you three, I wouldn't be here right now."

"We would do anything to keep you safe, darlin'. You don't have to thank us."

"I want to. I love you all so much. I don't understand how I can feel the way I do after only knowing you for such a short time, but I do."

"Give her to me," Rylan demanded and scooped Alyson out of Tarkyn's arms. "We were fated to meet, baby. Don't question it, just accept it. We love you, too, and we will enjoy teaching you everything you want about being a werewolf."

"As long as I don't have to be one."

"Not if we have anything to say about it," Chevy stated firmly. "Do you feel up to talking with Jarrod, darlin'? He wants to know what happened so he can write up a report."

"Okay, but can we do it outside? I don't want to be in here anymore."

Chevy looked around the dirty living room and motioned to Jarrod when their gazes met. His cousin gave a nod and followed them outside.

Everyone was there outside. They had arrived before Chevy and his brothers in case backup had been needed. Now they were all standing around the house, waiting to make sure their mate was safe.

Jonah came forward and stroked Alyson's hair in a comforting gesture. "Are you all right, Alyson?"

"Yes, thanks, Jonah. My men got to me in time."

Jonah nodded his head and gave one more scrutinizing look at Alyson and then moved off toward the house to speak with Malcolm.

Rylan sat down on the step, settling Alyson over his lap and pulling her close to his body. He nuzzled her neck with his nose and kissed her skin after breathing in her scent. Jarrod sat on the step next to them and took Alyson's statement.

By the time they were finished, his mate was struggling to keep her eyes open.

Rylan stood with her still in his arms. Chevy had been standing at the bottom of the steps, his knee bent so he was touching Alyson's leg, but now he straightened up as well, eager to get their mate back home. But before they'd gotten far, Jonah joined them again.

"You three did well in there," he said. "You were strong and courageous for your mate, and you acted smart by not letting your wolves take over. Thanks to you, that man will never threaten anyone again." The Alpha's eyes fell to Alyson and then lifted to Rylan. "That's why I want to make you my Betas."

Chevy saw Tarkyn begin smiling immediately. It took Rylan a little longer for the news to visibly sink in. "Your Betas?" he repeated. "So soon?"

Jonah put his hand on Rylan's shoulder, careful not to disturb Alyson. "I know you'll protect the rest of the pack as loyally as you protect your mate."

"Thank you, Alpha." Rylan bowed his head. Chevy and Tarkyn did likewise. "This is an honor."

Chevy could hear the pleasure in his brother's voice. He thanked Jonah as well, but it was hard to feel excited. *We have our promotion, but what about our mate?* Any other accomplishment would be hollow if Alyson wouldn't stay with them after all of this. After all, she was free now to go out on her own, independent and in no danger from Virgil.

"Here." Jarrod dug into his pocket and brought out the keys to his truck then handed them over to Tarkyn. "Take your mate home. I'll get a lift with Malcolm and Brax. And congratulations."

"Thank you." Tarkyn nodded to Rylan. "Let's go home."

Chevy followed them back to where all the vehicles had been parked out of sight. His anxieties came with him. *When Alyson wakes up, I guess we'll just have to see if she wants to stay.*

* * * *

Now that she was safe and her shock and adrenaline rush had passed, Alyson was exhausted. She could barely keep her eyes open and couldn't stop yawning. She was safe once more in the arms of one of her men. Rylan held her tight against him as he walked, the heat from his body warming her and his arms and muscles comforting. Placing her cheek against his shoulder, she let her eyes slide shut. Even though she was still aware of her men, she let her body drift in and out of a doze. The past few hours had been harrowing, and her body was demanding rest.

The closing of a door brought her up from her semiconscious state, and she opened her eyes and lifted her head just as Tarkyn started the sheriff's truck.

"Rest, baby. We'll be home before you know it, and then you can sleep."

"I want a shower. I need to wash his touch from my skin."

"Did he touch you, Aly?" Tarkyn asked from the driver's seat. "You never did say whether he touched you inappropriately while giving your statement to Jarrod."

"No, he didn't do..." She sobbed. "He just wanted to be able to see his work on my skin. He was going to cut me all over and then kill me."

"Shh, baby, you're safe now," Rylan whispered and caressed a hand up and down her thigh. "He won't ever be able to hurt you again."

"Virgil was going to torture me until I told him where his wife and child were." She buried her face in Rylan's chest. "I would have died before I betrayed them."

"Let me have her." Chevy reached out from his seat in the back next to her and Rylan. She could see the concern in his eyes and that need he had to hold her. Rylan passed her over, and Chevy hugged her tight, the sound of his heart beating and the weight of his arms and big body beneath her comforting. "We know you wouldn't have told that fucker where his family was hiding, Aly."

She sniffed and buried her face between his pectorals. His familiar scent and his muscular arms were just what she needed to push the last terrifying few hours from her mind. The drone of the truck's wheels on the road was soothing and her eyes closed once more. She relaxed into Chevy and let sleep take over her.

* * * *

"How is she?" Tarkyn looked into the rearview mirror and tried to see Alyson's face.

"She's asleep."

"Thank God. I think we should let her rest for as long as we can. We can help her clean up when she wakes, but I don't want to disturb her if she continues to sleep."

"I agree," Rylan said. "Our mate has been to hell and back and needs rest to recuperate."

"I want to kill the fucker over and over again for what he put our woman through." Tarkyn's voice came out in a deep rumble as his imagination replayed the knife plunging toward his mate. It was going to take some time before he got over his fear at seeing her naked and bound at the hands of Virgil Minogue.

He parked Jarrod's truck and got out, holding the rear door open for Chevy. When the women and some of the younger pack members surged out of the house, he placed his finger over his lips. Alyson needed to sleep, and he didn't want their voices waking her. Michelle came over and stood next to him, but instead of speaking out loud she used the pack common link.

"How is she really, Tarkyn?"

"She'll be fine. We got to her just in time. It may take her a while to get over the trauma, but she's safe and alive."

"Thank God. I heard you took that asshole out. You and your brothers are the perfect mates for her."

"Thank you, my queen." Tarkyn nodded his head in deference to his Alpha female.

"Cut that shit out, Tarkyn. You know I hate it. Sheesh." She smiled at him but cocked her hip with attitude.

"As you wish...Michelle."

"Get your woman upstairs to bed."

Chevy carried Alyson inside and upstairs to their suite of rooms and straight into Rylan's bed, since his was the largest. Rylan pulled the covers back, and he carefully laid her in the middle of the mattress. With gentle hands he and his brothers stripped their woman of her clothes and then took off their own before climbing into bed beside her. Rylan got in on her right, Tarkyn on her left, and Chevy lay across the bottom with a spare blanket to cover him. Rylan settled Alyson on her side and moved in until his front was plastered against hers with her head resting on his arm and shoulder. Tarkyn moved up against her back to spoon her, and Chevy wrapped an arm around her calf.

They were where they needed to be, breathing in their mate's scent and touching her, assuring themselves she was safe and sound. Alive, back where she belonged, in their beds, hearts, and souls.

* * * *

Alyson shifted in her sleep and whimpered. Rylan ran his hand up and down her side, soothing her, but she was so caught up in her nightmare she didn't respond to his touch. All of a sudden she bolted upright.

Tarkyn sat up and flicked the lamp on. Rylan reached out for Alyson, but she was still ensconced in her dream even though her eyes were open. Tears streamed down her face and her eyes darted around the room. She hit at him and cried out with terror.

He hugged her arms and upper torso so she couldn't hurt herself and lifted her onto his lap. Chevy and Tarkyn were talking to her, trying to get through to her and bring her out of her nightmare.

"It's all right, darlin', you're safe. We have you," Chevy crooned.

"Wake up, honey. We're here."

Nothing his brothers said made a difference. Alyson continued to struggle and cry.

"Wake up, Alyson!" Rylan yelled.

Her breathing hitched and she blinked several times. It seemed his loud voice had pulled her from her terror. Rylan eased his hold on her and wiped the moisture from her cheeks.

"That's it, baby. Wake up now. You're safe."

"Oh God," she sobbed. "I'm sorry. I didn't mean to wake you. Did I hurt you?"

Rylan snorted. "It would take a lot more than a hit from you to hurt me, baby. I'm a werewolf, remember."

Alyson pushed against his shoulder and arm. He released her, worried when she scrambled from the bed.

Alyson looked at all of them fearfully, as if they were strangers.

Rylan's heart ached for her. He wanted to comfort her, but his own fears choked him.

"What can we do for you, honey?" Chevy asked gently.

Alyson looked at them blankly. Rylan waited. *Don't pull away from us now.*

Chapter Fourteen

Alyson controlled her rampaging heart. The bad dream was fading away. She was safe, here with her men. But it wasn't enough.

Rylan followed her into the bathroom and rubbed her back as she washed her face and hands and then brushed her teeth. She headed out of the bathroom and paced around the room. Rylan leaned against the wall and watched her with a frown on his face. Alyson couldn't seem to settle down. Her insides were jumpy and her body felt shaky. She gripped her hands and tried to stop them shaking, but it didn't help. In fact, the harder she tried to stop the tremors the worse they were.

"Come here, Aly." Rylan pushed off from the wall and moved close to her. When he stopped in front of her he opened his arms, offering her comfort.

Alyson stepped into his embrace and shivered as his strong arms wrapped around her. The trembling intensified until she felt as if her legs were going to give out on her.

"Bring her back to bed," Tarkyn said.

Rylan carried her over to the bed and placed her in the center of the mattress and then climbed up next to her. Tarkyn reached over and pulled her into his arms until she was half lying on top of him with her head on his chest. Alyson's teeth were chattering, and she felt so cold she wondered if she would ever be warm again. And then their voices penetrated her hazy mind and she realized she was enfolded in the warmth of her three mates' bodies and their love.

"Shh, darlin', we've got you. You're safe, Aly. He can't ever hurt you again," Chevy said as he rubbed his hands up and down her legs as if trying to warm them.

"I've got you, honey. Just relax, Alyson. We will always keep you safe." Tarkyn's voice rumbled from his chest and against her ear.

Rylan kissed her neck and caressed a hand over her hip and thigh as he spoke, too. "We love you, Alyson. We are so sorry you got hurt. No one will ever get to you again, baby."

The shakes finally slowed and then stopped, but her men continued to surround her with their warmth and their love as well as crooning to her in low voices. But it wasn't enough.

When Rylan turned her to face him, she held on tight with her arms around his neck. She needed to feel their hands and mouths on her, loving her, wiping away the memory of Virgil's touch. Moving one arm up, she touched her palm to his cheek and stared deeply into his eyes. He shifted onto the bed until his body was covering hers, and she sighed with the bliss of his warm, hard frame blanketing her.

"I need you all. I love you so much," she sobbed. "Claim me and make me yours."

"Are you sure, baby?" Rylan asked. "That means you'll stay forever."

"Yes." That was exactly what she wanted. *Forever.* "Please. I want you to wipe his hands from my body."

"Shh, baby. We'll take care of you. Let us do all the work, baby. I don't want you hurting yourself." Rylan lowered his head and brushed his lips back and forth over hers. The reverent touch of his mouth expressed the love he felt for her in a profound way. The memories began to recede as her heart filled with emotion.

His cock hardened and lengthened against her mound and she pushed up, grinding her crotch into his. He groaned and deepened the kiss, opening and slanting his mouth over hers, thrusting his tongue in and tasting her. Alyson slid her tongue over and around his, feeling his desire as his addictive essence exploded on her tongue.

Rylan wrapped his arms around her and rolled over onto his side, taking her with him. Another set of hands caressed up and down her back, and she knew by his unique scent that Chevy was behind her.

He moved her hair aside and kissed, licked, and nibbled his way down her neck and shoulders.

Tarkyn had moved down the bed near her feet and began to rub his hands up and down her thighs and over the cheeks of her ass. Then he lifted one of her legs and placed it over Rylan's hip. His breath rasped over her pussy and clit, causing the sensitive bundle of nerves to throb for more. Her pussy leaked continuously, preparing to be filled. Rylan withdrew from her mouth, and she gasped in air as he kissed his way down her chest. He licked around one areola and then the other, teasing her skin until it gathered in and her nipples hardened. She arched up, begging him without words to suck the protruding tips, and he gave a chuckle before finally sucking one turgid peak into his mouth.

As his wet heat enfolded her, pleasure swamped her and zinged straight down to her pussy. She cried out when Tarkyn licked through her wet folds and then sobbed with frustration as he pulled away again. But then he spread her labial lips wide with his fingers and bent to her again, placing his mouth at her hole and slurping up her juices. He moved back up to the top of her slit and flicked his tongue up and down over her clit.

Alyson clutched Rylan's head and held him to her breast as he began to lave the other nipple. Chevy lifted one of her ass cheeks and caressed her anus with cool, wet fingers. She was on an overload of sensation, and she didn't want them to stop. Never had she felt so connected to another human being as she did to each of these men. Her heart was so full of emotion that she wanted to shout to the world how much she loved and needed these three men.

Chevy pushed a finger into her rosette and then began to slowly fuck her ass. Tarkyn eased a finger into her cunt, and he, too, pumped in and out of her while his tongue worked her clit. But it still wasn't enough. She needed more. Alyson wanted her mates to make love to her together. One in her mouth, another in her ass, and the third in her vagina. Just as that thought coalesced, her men stopped and withdrew.

"We are going to love you now, baby. Are you ready?" Rylan asked, his voice deep and husky.

"God yes. Please? I need you so much."

Rylan picked her up and carried her over to the sofa near the window. He sat up in the corner with the arm at his back and pulled her on top of him.

"Take me inside you, baby." He gripped the base of his cock and held it up for her.

Alyson maneuvered until she was above him and slowly sank down onto him. They both groaned as her wet pussy enveloped his dick to the hilt. He held on to her hips and kept her still when she would have begun to move over him.

Chevy moved in close to her back on his knees and drizzled more lube down the crack of her ass.

"Take a couple of deep breaths for me, darlin'. Just relax and let us love you."

Alyson did as he said and then moaned when he rubbed the head of his cock up and down over her puckered entrance. Then he was pushing forward, and the head of his erection penetrated her ass. He held still for a moment, and she canted her hips to give him better access. She released another breath, and that helped to relax her muscles, allowing him to surge forward with one thrust until he was balls-deep inside her.

Legs brushed against her side as Tarkyn climbed over the back of the sofa and sat on the top. He was in the perfect position for her to get her mouth on him if she turned her head. Leaning over slightly, she licked up his cock from the base to the tip and then around the corona. He tasted so good, salty yet sweet, and she craved more.

Opening her mouth, she sucked him in between her lips and went down on him as far as she could without gagging, then she drew back up. Each time she swallowed his cock she increased the pace, until she was bobbing up and down his shaft. Her mouth made slurping sounds, and she hummed around his flesh when she tasted more pre-cum on her tongue.

"Fuck, honey. Your mouth feels so damn good. Hum on me some more. The vibrations feel like heaven." Tarkyn panted.

As she got into a rhythm, humming every now and then to enhance Tarkyn's pleasure, Chevy and Rylan started to move. First Chevy pulled back, and as he surged forward, Rylan withdrew. Her pussy gushed out more cream as their cocks massaged the walls of her ass and cunt.

With every thrust and pump of their hips they increased the pace until their flesh was slapping against hers. Taking a deep breath and relaxing her throat, Alyson took Tarkyn's cock way down until her lips reached the base of his penis. She held still and then hummed and swallowed around him.

"Shit. If you keep that up, honey, I'll be coming in seconds." Tarkyn groaned.

Alyson whimpered. Her internal walls flexed and rippled as Rylan and Chevy pounded in and out of her holes. And then a slap landed on one of her ass cheeks and then the other. He smacked her butt five more times on each side, which only seemed to enhance her pleasure. The heat spread out and the vibrations traveled to her clit, causing the little bud to throb incessantly.

"When you're better, we are going to spank this sexy ass some more," Chevy rasped as he surged forward.

"If you ever goad someone into killing you again," Rylan panted as he slid his cock nearly all the way out, "you won't sit down for a week."

"You are in so much trouble, honey. We aren't ever letting you go now," Tarkyn groaned as she sucked on his cock.

Her muscles began to coil and gather in, and she knew she was close to her peak, but she wanted at least one of her men to climax before she did. Reaching out, she cupped Tarkyn's balls in the palm of her hand and then rolled them around in their sac as she licked the sensitive underside with her tongue. He gasped and threaded his fingers into her hair, wrapping it around his wrist.

"I'm gonna come, Aly."

She slid down over his cock until it touched the back of her throat and swallowed as she lightly squeezed his balls. Tarkyn yelled as his balls drew up to his body and then he shot load after load of cum into her mouth and throat. She moaned as she tasted his semen and drank it down with relish, loving his taste and knowing she had brought him pleasure. He withdrew his softening cock from her mouth and then kissed her long and hard.

Her body began to shake as tingling warmth heated her blood and flowed through her veins. Her muscles tautened to the point of pain, and she gripped Rylan's shoulders as he shoved his cock into her pussy deeply.

"Fuck. Your ass is squeezing me tighter than a fist," Chevy rasped. "I'm close, darlin'. Rylan, send her over."

Alyson mewled when Rylan slid a hand down her stomach and caressed her clit. The warmth turned into an inferno. She screamed as ecstasy washed over her. Her pussy clenched and released around his cock while her ass clamped down on Chevy's penis. The bliss of her orgasm shot her into the stratosphere, her body shaking and shuddering with nirvana.

Rylan licked the skin where her shoulder and neck met, once, twice, three times, and then white-hot, pleasurable pain pierced her flesh as he sank his teeth into her. From behind her, Chevy did the same. It was one of the biggest, longest orgasms she'd experienced.

Rylan slowly removed his teeth from her shoulder and licked the wound he had made. At once, Tarkyn bit the spot just beside his brother's mark. Pain radiated into her shoulders, but it only amped up her desire even more. She climaxed again.

Her ears were ringing along with her rapture. Alyson was only vaguely aware of the shouts Rylan and Chevy gave as they reached climax and pumped her body full of their cum.

When the last wave faded, she slumped against Rylan, secure in the knowledge that her mates wouldn't let her fall. She felt connected to each of the three men and wanted to hold on to them and never let go. It felt like there was a thread connecting her heart to each of theirs and vice versa. She was covered with sweat and sticky from their lovemaking, but she didn't care. She was safe and loved in the arms of her men, and she would be for the rest of her life.

Now that the danger was over, she had so much to look forward to, but one thing was certain. She had found love when she'd least expected it, and she was going to hold on to that love and her men for years to come.

"I love you, baby."

Alyson sat up and saw the love shining from Rylan's eyes. "I love you, too."

Chevy eased his softening cock from her ass, causing them both to groan, and lifted her from Rylan's lap. He kissed her softly on the lips.

"I love you, darlin'."

"Me, too." She stroked his cheek with her palm and smiled and then reached out for Tarkyn. "I love you, Tarkyn."

"That's a good thing, honey, because you're stuck with us." Tarkyn took her from Chevy and headed to the bathroom. "Let's get you cleaned up so you can sleep some more."

"I don't want to sleep. I want to spend the rest of the night making love with my men." She gave him a sultry look and then gripped his cock after he let her feet down to the floor.

"Oh you do, do you?" Tarkyn gave her a lopsided grin and waggled his eyebrows. "We'll let you get away with telling us what to do just this once."

"Oh, you are so full of it." His cock had already begun to fill with blood once more. "You want me just as much as I want you."

"Yes, we do, baby," Rylan said as he hugged her from behind. "But just remember, we like to be in control in the bedroom."

"How could I forget that?" she asked. "You three move me every which way, and there is nothing I can do about it but let you have your way."

"And you just hate that, don't you, darlin'," Chevy said as he entered the bathroom and lifted her arms above her head before sucking one of her nipples into his mouth.

After they washed up, Tarkyn carried her back to the bedroom and sat her on the side of the bed. He and Chevy knelt down in front of her and held her hands. She looked up as Rylan came out of the bathroom and joined them. He, too, knelt before her.

Rylan cupped her cheek, careful not to touch her bruises or the swelling on her face, and stared deeply into her eyes. "Will you marry us, Alyson? We know how important marriage is to humans. We want to make our bond legal in the eyes of their law, too."

Her heart stuttered, and then tears of joy streamed from her eyes. She didn't know who she would be marrying on paper and she realized it would be only one of her men, but she didn't care. In her heart she was already married to these three wonderful, loving, dominant, protective men.

"Yes. God, yes a thousand times over."

Her men threw their heads back and howled with joy. She looked down when she felt a ring being slid onto her finger. It was stunning.

"It's beautiful. Thank you all so much."

"That ring belonged to our grandmother, baby. She wanted us to give it to our mate. We're so glad you like it."

A ruby sat in the center with a diamond on either side, set in yellow gold. Rylan, Tarkyn, and Chevy all hugged her at once. She could feel their love surrounding her.

Alyson exhaled, tears still running down her face. She was finally where she was meant to be, wrapped up in the arms of the loves of her life.

THE END

WWW.BECCAVAN-EROTICROMANCE.COM

ABOUT THE AUTHOR

My name is Becca Van. I live in Australia with my wonderful hubby of many years, as well as my two children.

I read my first romance, which I found in the school library, at the age of thirteen and haven't stopped reading them since. It is so wonderful to know that love is still alive and strong when there seems to be so much conflict in the world.

I dreamed of writing my own book one day but, unfortunately, didn't follow my dream for many years. But once I started I knew writing was what I wanted to continue doing.

I love to escape from the world and curl up with a good romance, to see how the characters unfold and conflict is dealt with. I have read many books and love all facets of the romance genre, from historical to erotic romance. I am a sucker for a happy ending.

For all titles by Becca Van, please visit
www.bookstrand.com/becca-van

Siren Publishing, Inc.
www.SirenPublishing.com

CPSIA information can be obtained at www.ICGtesting.com
Printed in the USA
LVOW09s1755220215

427898LV00026B/898/P